Sunshine Country

Sunshine Country

Kristiny Royovej

Christian Focus Publications

This edition copyright © 2003
Christian Focus Publications

ISBN 1-85792-855-5

Published by
Christian Focus Publications Ltd
Geanies House, Fearn, Tain, Ross-shire
IV20 1TW, Scotland, Great Britain.

www.christianfocus.com
email: info@christianfocus.com

Cover Illustration by Murillo
Cover design by Catherine Mackenzie

Printed and bound in Great Britain
by Cox & Wyman, Reading.

Contents

Introduction

Miss Cristina Roy, whose name appears on the title page of this book, is in charge of an orphanage in Czechoslovakia, whose origin was largely due to inspiration received from the Orphan Homes of Bristol, founded by George Müller. It was for the benefit of this home of hers that the story was originally published in the Slovak language. The interest it created was sufficient to cause its translation into German, French and Spanish, and then from this Spanish version, the present writer has re-translated the story into his mother tongue, feeling that there is a strong message for the English people.

The story is founded on actual facts, and those who may wish to locate the territory covered in the events will find it without difficulty in the mountainous region and winding valley watered by the River Wag.

W.M.S.

Palko

After a long hard winter, with heavy snow and keen frost, spring had arrived in all its beauty. No one greeted it with greater pleasure than little Palko Juriga. Like a bird escaped from its cage he set forth from the village, and started up the path that led to his beloved mountains. Life at school and in the little old house in the village during the long winter had been very confined. Even the windows of the houses, from autumn to spring had been stopped up with moss to keep out the cold.

Old Pablo Juriga, whose surname had been given to Palko, was neither his father nor his grandfather, but this had not kept them from loving one another, and Palko always called the old gentleman Grandfather. Palko's grandfather, Juriga, worked in the mountains during the summer months making flour sieves. There, away in the heart of the green hills, he owned his little hut which, after being cleaned each spring, had been his summer dwelling for nearly thirty years. At first his children had stayed with him, but, like the young eagles of the surrounding crags, they had flown far from the paternal nest. So the old man had formed the custom of choosing a companion from among those who came to cut wood in the mountains. The wood was in great demand, for many wood-workers arrived in the villages during the summer and they had need of it. Two years before our story opens, a man named Rasga, about the same age as Juriga, had come to share the hut with him, accompanied by a little boy.

His health, however, had broken down through rough work, and, perhaps, also by the severe climate of the mountains. He coughed constantly, and was unable to do much work. The little boy who had come with him attended him like a devoted son. He chopped firewood, gathered mushrooms, boiled the soup, and did what he could to make life easier for his aged companion. One day poor old Rasga took to his bed, and a few days later he said to Juriga: "My friend, you have no one in the world to take care of you, and this little boy is in the same condition. As for me, I am going home to die, and I do not wish to take the boy back with me, for I do not know of anyone there who will look after him when I am gone. Keep him here, for he will prove useful to you, as he has been to me."

"I should be glad to have him, but what will his parents say?" Asked Juriga, running his hand through his few grey hairs.

"Listen," said Rasga, having sent the boy to the mountainside to gather a few mushrooms, "this lad is not my grandson, as you suppose, and I don't even know if his parents are living. He came into the care of my dear daughter in a very strange way a few years before her death. Stop working for a minute, while I tell you his story." Juriga obeyed, and what his friend told him impressed itself on his memory.

"One day my daughter Anna was gathering mushrooms on the mountain, when suddenly she thought she heard the cry of a child. You know how timid and superstitious women are — they always fear the devil is trying to trap them — and so she paid no heed to the sound. But the child's crying continued. She herself had two young children, so she went into the densest part of the forest, where the sound of crying came from, and there she found a little lad, about two years old, who ran sobbing towards her, almost blue with cold for he was dressed only in a little shirt. How he came to be in such a lonely place, and who could have left him there, it was impossible to find out, for the child knew only the one word, 'Mamma.' Anna took him in her arms and wrapped her shawl about him, dried his tears and gave him something to eat and drink, having a piece of bread in her pocket. The poor little fellow ate like a hungry dog, and then he slept the sleep of exhaustion in her arms. His hair and the little shirt were saturated with dew, a sign that he had passed the whole night in the forest without shelter.

"I have asked myself many times since, who watched over him and protected him from wild beasts of the forest? For there are many wild boars inhabiting that region."

"The children certainly have their guardian angels," said Juriga as tears came to his eyes.

For some minutes both men remained silent, thinking of the lost child wandering on the mountainside, perhaps finally sobbing himself to sleep on a bank of moss—alone, and far from his mother's arms.

"What happened after that?" asked Pablo.

"Anna brought him home to us, and, having recently buried a little one named Palko, she gave this same name to the foundling. Weeks and months rolled by and we could discover nothing about his parents. My son-in-law, at that time an excellent person of good habits, was agreeable to the adoption of the boy; but my daughter Anna died when Palko was about five years of age, and the new wife, who soon came to take her place, is not even a good mother to her own children —

11

so the poor little stranger came to be simply a 'thorn in the flesh'. For that reason I, in a sense, adopted him myself, and sent him off to school with the idea of keeping him clear of the house, but he took good advantage of that opportunity, for by the end of the first winter he had learned to read. You can be sure of one thing, that is, that his parents, whoever and whatever they are, are persons of character and intelligence. I know very well, if I die, the people at my house will send him out to tend geese somewhere, and he will forget all his learning. So take him, friend Juriga! The lad will surely be useful to you. Besides, I cannot but believe that the day will come when his parents will come to claim him, and you will be able to say to them that he has been well cared for in my house—that what I had was shared with him, and when my grandchildren had to suffer from the bad temper of their foster mother, and when my son-in-law began to drink and be cruel to everybody in the house, I took Palko under my protection. 'Tis well if they give thanks to God for protecting their son! I have never told Palko these things nor how he was found. I have never thought it wise to do so. Tell me, Juriga, will you not let the lad stay with you?"

"Indeed I will, friend Rasga, and I will send him to school. In the summer-time he shall stay here with me to serve his apprenticeship, and I will teach him to make sieves and wooden spoons, and then in the winter off he shall go to school."

So Rasga took his departure after leaving the little boy in Juriga's care. At first Palko cried bitterly over the departure of his grandfather, but Juriga took his place so well that Palko soon dried his tears and became his old happy self.

Now, as our story opens, another year-and-a-half have passed, and the old man and Palko feel as if they had lived together always.

Today, Palko has skipped on ahead, climbing the slope of the mountain instead of keeping to the path. He wants to sweep and tidy the hut before his grandfather arrives. The bundle on his back contains a change of clothing, a large loaf of bread, some onions, smoked meat and potatoes, and a bit of salt done up in paper. Besides this, there hangs from his shoulder a small bundle of his grandfather's tools; there is an earthen jug in one hand and his staff in the other. Palko marches on with a light step, for he feels as happy as a prince. A dented old hat tries to cover a mass of curly yellow hair, and a little dark red cape, bordered with blue, protects his shoulders; pantaloons of homespun cloth, a shirt with wide sleeves; carefully adjusted grass sandals, and a belt of black leather with bright brass buckles complete his costume. His great, dark-blue eyes are just now shining with joy. "O Liberty, Liberty, Liberty, how precious thou art!" It is an old song of Czechoslovakia— well he sings it, for his very being dances as the sheer joy of living pipes its lively rhythm.

"Hallo!" he shouts at the mountains, and back the echo comes: "HALLO! Hallo! Hallo! Hallo! Hallo!"

"You-ou! You-ou!" and Palko laughs happily as the echo throws back his laugh at him. Whoever would have believed that the mountains would give him such a welcome!

"Good-morning, son of mine. You here already?" said a voice from behind him. It was Liska, the woodcutter.

"Good morning, little uncle,"* said Palko,

(*a Slavic mode of salutation)

stretching out his hand, for Liska was an old friend. "I've come on ahead to get the hut ready."

"It will be a miracle if the winter snow hasn't knocked it down. Well, I must be getting on. See you later," said Liska. "I'm away to the forest guard's house."

The higher Palko climbed the more numerous became the huts, and from many of the chimneys columns of smoke were already ascending—a sign that some people had already arrived in the woods. Other huts were but broken timbers wrecked by the snow, which still partly covered them. It was necessary to cross several brooks greatly swollen by the slowly melting snows, and the only green that showed on the mountainside were the pine and hemlock trees, for the rest of the forest had just begun to bud.

At last our young traveller has arrived at his destination, for there, at a turn in the road, is the hut—his hut and Juriga's. How his eyes light with joy to find it undamaged in spite of the hard winter! Although built only of wood and clay, the humble little dwelling appeared to him a palace. Was it not his home? Besides, how wonderful to find it undamaged by the winter snows, just as they had left it in the autumn.

Grabbing a birch broom from a corner, Palko swept the floor and arranged the fire on the hearth in the centre of the cabin, with a bundle of firewood and some twigs to start it with. Then he put in their proper places all the things he had brought with him. This done, he ran to the spring and filled his jug from the crystal water that came out of the hill close to the hut.

"Well done, my son!" exclaimed his grandfather who, at that moment, entered the little dwelling.

Very soon Palko had his potatoes peeled and in the little three-legged pot which was boiling over the fire. "Prepare the stew, my son," instructed Juriga, "while I go after some dried leaves which I spied near here, and which will do well for a bed."

The twigs crackled merrily under the pot, illuminating the earnest face of the busy little cook. Into the water went salt, then a little butter, followed by a handful of cumin seed, then a few onions, and some slices of dry bread. Soon the feast was ready and off came the little pot from the fire.

"Grandfather! Grandfather, the stew is ready!" Palko shouted from the door.

"I'm coming, I'm coming, son of mine!" and soon the old man entered, carrying a heavy load of dried leaves in a great sack which he laid in a corner.

From his pockets he took two wooden spoons, and he and Palko were soon using them with very great enjoyment. You could not find the recipe for that stew in any cookery book, but to them it was as food for kings.

The feast finished, their soft rustic bed was quickly arranged. The sun at that moment seemed to poise itself just above the mountaintop, so the little boy and the old workman prepared to rest for a while. Palko threw an old sheepskin over his grandfather, wrapped himself in his little cloak, and before you could count fifty, they were asleep. The fire still burned in the middle of the hut, the smoke going up through a hole in the roof, mixing itself with the scent of the pines. Everywhere throughout the valley there breathed the atmosphere of spring, from the soil, from the plants, and from the trees.

In a few days the whole mountain began to teem

with life and animation. From early morning till late at night the sounds could be heard of the click-chop, click-chop of the axes, the crash of trees falling to earth, the swish of the great two-hand saws, the crackle of the branches as they broke and the thunder of the logs as the piles rose in the forest. Added to all this was the murmur of human voices. It would have been better that many of these should not have been heard at all, for coarse jests rose from many of these throats. Strange indeed that, in the midst of this beautiful scene of God's blessing, men should act like this!

Soon all the huts were filled with workers, many of whom appeared as if they were beings without souls, committing acts at times that placed them below the level of animals. There were, however, a few decent and worthy men, among whom were Liska and Juriga, although an oath would escape their lips once in a while.

But one person who inspired the greatest response among all that rough group of men was Palko, and as he was the only boy among them, he was considered a sort of common treasure so that it became necessary, in their opinion, to suppress an oath or unseemly joke when Palko came near. He was a great favourite, ever ready to help and do whatever might be required by any one of his many acquaintances, such as carrying water and acting as general man-of-all-work. He would gather strawberries on the mountain and distribute them to all his friends on the way back to the hut.

Juriga saw with pleasure this lovely trait in the boy's character, that toward everyone he met he showed the same simplicity and whole-hearted confidence, so that the old man used to apply to Palko an old Slavic proverb: 'Gentlemen were made to be gentlemen as the mountains were made to be mountains.' He himself as a young man had been held in high esteem for the same frankness and openness of character, and even now he lived happily with his neighbours. As he himself said: "No one has ever been able to complain of my treatment of them, I never do harm to anyone. I greet them all alike with civility and courtesy; if any lack salt, cereals, butter, or tobacco, I lend him willingly, and I am taking care of this child purely out of love to God." Juriga had never heard the story of the self-righteous Pharisee and, therefore, was more than satisfied with his own virtues.

The Sunshine Country

On a certain Sunday in the month of May some of our mountain friends had descended to the village to attend church, others to seek work of the municipal authorities, and a great number to visit the tavern— a sort of combination of general store and liquor shop. Here most of the wood-workers spent Sunday and the greater part of their hard-earned money in strong drink. Those that remained on the mountainside slept a good part of the day or set out to look for strawberries. Seated in the sunshine at his doorway, old Juriga rested, when suddenly he heard footsteps and the barking of a dog. A hunter, perhaps, thought Juriga but, but he was wrong, it was only a young fellow, apparently a new arrival.

"Good morning, sir," said the stranger. "Do you live alone here?"

"Only my little grandson and I. Why did you wish to know?"

"I must work here for a few weeks, and thought, perhaps, you might give me accommodation."

"Very good, but what is your work?"

"I'm a wood-turner by trade. May I come and leave my bundle here?"

"Yes, why not? And now you have to return to the village?"

"No, only to the forest-keeper's where my things are. Tomorrow I will come back."

"Very well, sir. You've come at a good time. Sit down for a bit. Is the dog yours?"

"Yes, come here, Dunaj!" The dog, pure white, in one bound came to his master's side. "I had shut him up in the house, but he found a way out and here he is."

"What is your name, sir?"

"Martin Lesina."

More than content to have someone to talk to, Juriga asked the stranger an endless string of questions concerning the city from whence he came, how the people lived there, the state of cultivation, and so on. Martin, for his part, was put wise to all that was going on in the forest life around the cottage in order that he might not be deceived by anyone.

"I am very short of money," said Martin, "and that is the reason I have come to cut wood for myself, instead of ordering it as I usually do. I am, therefore, grateful to you for your good counsel, and will see you tomorrow."

"I think that chap's all right," remarked Pablo to himself, as he watched his new acquaintance disappear through the forest. "He's as straight as a pine, and it's easy to see he's been a soldier, and mighty intelligent, too! Nevertheless, in spite of his youth, he has a sad look about him, as of one who has nothing to hope for in this life. But, where is Palko? He will be happy over the dog, especially such a beauty! What can have kept him so long?"

The little boy had gone out early that morning looking for mushrooms. He had wandered far away up the mountain seeking the best places, and soon had quite a load. When Palko was ready to return, it occurred to him that as it was Sunday there was no particular reason to hurry home. He was very anxious to discover what might be on the other side of that towering mass of rock at the top of the mountain. As he had looked at it day after day he had said to himself many times: "I wonder what kind of world it is that is hidden away on the other side."

In bygone days, when his little Mother Anna was living, she used to tell him such delightful stories. One story in particular he had made her tell him over and over again. It was about a king who had disappeared, and whose son had wandered everywhere seeking his father. One day, on arriving at a certain range of mountains, he saw an immense rock in front of him, and presently a golden-winged bird flew near and whispered in his ear, telling him to climb the rock, and assuring him that on the other side he would find a wonderful land called the Sunshine Country, where the sun never, never went down; and that there also he should find his father the king. The boy at once began to climb, but many great monsters came out to bar his path. One was a serpent, another a lion, and then a bear. But there came also to help him a most valiant knight in shining armour, mounted on a fiery steed, who put to flight his enemies and carried the little boy on his horse to the royal palace in the Sunshine Country, where he found his long-lost father, the king.

In the village school Palko had questioned the teacher as to where he could find the Sunshine Country where the sun never went down, for he did not seem to be able to find it on his map. His teacher replied, laughing, that he would find it in the Land of Stories, which did not appear anywhere in geography.

How many times since then had Palko desired to find that Land of Stories. "Now, who knows," thought Palko, "perhaps it might be there behind that great peak in front of me, with its head shrouded in a cloud like the hood over the head of the monk I saw in the the town."

"Today I have the time and I am going." Leaving his load of mushrooms where he could easily find it on his return, Palko began to climb the steep path that led to the peak.

"Surely it must be there on the other side," he said to himself, impatient to arrive at the top, "I've seen the sun disappear so many times behind that peak and I know it never sets in the Sunshine Country, so there's no night there, and it must be warm always." With the exertion of climbing he began to feel hot already.

Finally, on arrival at the top of that last and highest crag, he saw at his feet on the other side, a beautiful valley completely enclosed by mountains on all sides and flooded throughout with the sunshine of a May day. The great rock on which he stood slanted downwards in a series of steeply-graded terraces to the bottom of the valley, where, like a beautiful green carpet, there lay a huge green field as if full of violets. From the rock itself flowed a crystal spring that descended into the valley, like a silver-plated serpent, bordered with rosebushes and wild cherries.

In contrast with the sombre forest he had left behind, silence did not reign here. The blackbirds called, the chaffinches and thrushes answered, and the squirrels hopped about everywhere. Such a stirring, such animation, and abundant life showed on all sides.

"Yes, indeed!" said Palko joyfully to himself. "This must be the Sunshine Country!"

To study better all these marvels spread out before his eyes, he placed his foot carefully on a stone a little below the ledge. Just then he saw an astonishing thing. Down where the little spring sprang from the mountain was what appeared to be a hole in the rock. He scrambled down to find that the opening was so small he could enter only on all fours. Happily, through a cleft above, a stray beam of sunshine allowed one to see the interior. The little cave apparently was, or had been, a dwelling place for someone, for in the middle of it was a table and a bench. From the walls hung cobwebs, and on the floor a quantity of dry moss was gathered, brought in by the wind.

"It's a dwelling sure enough!" exclaimed Palko, "I wonder who lives here?"

He entered, not without a thrill, and spied something on the table — a book!

Opening it, Palko began to read the words he found written on the first page:

'Whoever you are, you that takes this sacred volume in your hand — read it with perseverance and attention, line after line. It shall teach you the Way that leads from this vale of tears to the country where there is no night and where the sun never goes down, the land of light and happiness eternal!'

It was true! He had not been mistaken! This mysterious little black book would show him the road to the Sunshine Country! So it existed after all, really and truly, even though it couldn't be found in the map at school. Palko seated himself and, with hands supporting his head, began to read. He had a great desire to skip the first page, for it contained nothing but a string of names of men and women; but the words written on the inside of the front cover said that the book should be read line after line.

The names were probably those of the country he was seeking, and such strange names they were; but of course, no doubt quite common where they lived. After these came some well-known names, Joseph and Mary, and then a beautiful name, Emmanuel, which it seemed meant 'God with us'.

Then the book said that a boy had been born, and they had given him the name of Jesus. What a beautiful name, even more so than Emmanuel. Palko had heard often the expression, 'Jesus be praised' as used by his neighbours, and also in moments of sudden fear, 'Jesus, Mary and Joseph!' Could they be the same ones spoken of in the book? 'Lord God, help me!' So said his grandfather in certain critical moments, and so now did Palko, and then proceeded with this reading. What followed was not so difficult to understand. The book told how, at the birth of Jesus in Bethlehem, there was a certain man named Herod, who appeared to be the king of the country. Some wise men came to the king, desirous of seeing this wonderful baby. What was this star they had seen in the East, which seemed to have something to do with the boy they wanted to see? But no one was able to show them, they just followed the star until it stopped over a house in Bethlehem, and there in that very house they found the boy Jesus. It would be some enchanted prince, seeing that they fell on their knees before him, and filled with great awe and respect, offered him gold, frankincense and myrrh. (These last two gifts, would they be, perhaps, some kind of food?) After this they returned to their own land by an entirely different road, for God had ordered them so to do.

"O how beautiful it all is!" exclaimed the boy, clapping his hands with delight. "This man Herod was like a dragon that wanted to devour the boy Jesus, but he couldn't for an angel came by night and made them all go away, Mary, Joseph and the boy. What a kind gentleman Joseph was, but what a terrible thing happened then, when the terrible dragon man killed all the children, and the mothers cried as if they could never be comforted. How many things I have learned today about the Sunshine Country! But I must be content with this, otherwise grandfather will be worried about me. After all, it's not so far away from home, and I can come back every day, every Sunday anyway. I do so want to know what happened to the enchanted prince and also to discover for myself the road to the Sunshine Country."

Palko has a Secret

Five weeks had scarcely passed since Martin Lesina had come to live with Juriga, but it seemed to them as if he had always been there. Juriga was not mistaken in saying that Palko would be more than delighted with the dog's company. In fact, the pleasure was entirely mutual and, wherever the marks of the little boy's sandals were found, one was sure to see the dog's footprints also.

From the time of Martin's arrival, Juriga went no more to the tavern with the other woodcutters because Martin neither drank nor smoked. "Once, when I was in a drunken state," said Martin, "a terrible thing happened, of which I do not even care to speak." This was the reply which Juriga received when he invited his new friend to accompany him to the tavern. Then he added to Juriga: "And you yourself would do well also in quitting the drink. With what we should save in that way we could have milk every day and meat on Sundays."

The suggestion pleased Juriga very much. He did not care so much for meat, but was very, very fond of milk. Previously he had never been able to satisfy his desire except once in a while, but now he could have either hot or cold milk when he pleased. However, he could not seem to do without his pipe, and occasionally Martin brought him tobacco. Life was good and Martin became like a son to our Juriga. Palko had his bed in another corner of the hut, where he had the happiest of dreams in the world in the company of Dunaj, the dog.

There was only one thing which appeared strange to Juriga. Martin, who showed himself so pleasant to everybody — and he was, surely, a man of learning — hardly ever looked at Palko, and yet the lad, as usual, always helped him when necessary. The old man had not noticed that Palko did not chatter as much as usual. He seemed to take great pleasure in going for the milk, and often returned very late and very tired. It was not difficult to see, also, that Dunaj had done his share of running. Juriga would surely have noticed this if he had been alone, but, taken up with Martin's company, he did not think much about Palko. For three Sundays in succession the men went to church, not returning until nightfall, and finding the meal prepared, it did not occur to them to ask Palko what he had been doing with himself all day.

It is no small thing for a boy to have a secret—and such a secret! Why did he not say anything about his precious treasure? Palko would not have been able to explain this even to himself, but he remembered certain stories in which, when the people spoke of what they had seen, the whole thing disappeared. If he told anyone that he had actually discovered one of the outposts of the Sunshine Country, with its mysterious grotto and the holy book; that he went there for a little while every day, and on Sunday stayed from morning till night to read line after line in order to find the road to the true Sunshine Country, who knew but that the grotto might disappear with the book and all the rest of it? In that case he would never be able to learn what he wanted to know.

Therefore, he kept quiet about his great secret, and he would rather suffer punishment for having spent too much time in search of strawberries than reveal the true cause of his delay. When the day arrived that he knew all he desired, he would share his secret with his grandfather, and then they would both journey together to the country where this boy Jesus lived.

Nevertheless, as he advanced in his reading, he thought less and less about the kingdom of stories. His one desire was to know more and more about Jesus. Jesus — how great was his kindness! How wonderful his power! He seemed to be able to do anything he wished, because he was God's Son. Palko understood little of what happened on the banks of the Jordan between Jesus and John, that strange man who ate only locusts and wild honey. One thing he did understand, a great voice sounded from heaven, and, being from heaven, it was God's voice that made men understand that Jesus was his beloved Son whom it was necessary to obey. In the Slavic language the same word is used for 'to hear' and 'to obey'.

But how could that be? Joseph, then, was not his father? "Ah, yes, I understand, it's the same with Juriga, who is not my true grandfather, but he takes care of me, the people believe that I am his grandson, and so they believed that Joseph was Jesus' father."

Palko was immediately convinced that now he must obey the commands of the Lord Jesus for had not the Father God ordered it so?

"When I understand fully," he said to himself, "what Jesus had to say to the people, then I, too, will obey him even though I may not be able to see him personally." Oh, how powerful he was! How well he understood how to overcome the devil when he tried to tempt him! And another wonderful thing, how he called sinners to himself, taught them and healed all the sick that came to him to be cured! Then how he gave bread to the hungry poor people, even bread enough to feed thousands of people! How many wonderful things there were in the book. But what is going to happen now, seeing that many people begin to turn against him?

What sad things did Palko now have to read? How difficult he found it to sleep at night, owing to the fact that his imagination brought the whole thing before him so vividly. That terrible night in the garden where Jesus prayed, and where he was in such agony that he sweated great drops of blood. And then — to think of it — his disciples slept instead of watching with him! "If I had been there, I would have put my arms about his neck and said, 'Fear not, God will save thee!'"

But he didn't save him! Why? Why didn't he deliver him from his enemies? These wicked men came and took him and after that—and the tears almost made it impossible for Palko to read on. How they flogged him and put him to shame, and at last nailed him to the cross. "I hadn't the least idea that the Christ in front of the church on a wooden cross was this same Lord Jesus. Of course, it isn't really him personally, but just a mere image. But now at least I know that they crucified him! If only I could know why! Oh, why did God not liberate him when he cried: 'My God! My God! Why hast thou forsaken me?' instead of letting him die? And then they buried him!"

Palko closed the book and went away sorely puzzled. The sun was still high above the horizon, the mountain still wore its holiday dress, with its green forest lands and lovely flowers; Dunaj capered about happily, chasing squirrels and birds. Palko alone could not rejoice.

"What good are all these flowers? How can these little birds sing, when Jesus is dead?" thought the boy. "As he no longer lives, I shall never be able to see him, nor be able to tell him how much I care for him, and that I had decided to do what he said."

The following day he didn't return to the cave. Nevertheless, there came to his mind the words on the first page of the book, line after line. If he wished to know the road to the Sunshine Country, he must read still further. Besides, he wanted to know what Mary and the disciples did when Jesus was no longer with them. Sunday had come again, the third Sunday that Juriga and Martin had spent in the town. Seated in the grotto, his head in his hands, Palko was absorbed in his reading. Then all of a sudden he rose and jumped for joy.

"He lives! He lives!" cried Palko, and from far away across the valley the echo came back: "He lives! He lives!"

Always ready to join with his young master in all his moods, the dog scampered toward him, wagging his tail.

"Dunaj! Jesus is living now, do you know? He is God's Son! The stone was rolled away and he had come to life again. Now, leave me alone so that I can read what follows. I must know what happened afterward, and I'll tell you all about it later." The dog obeyed, and Palko seated himself again and was soon deep in his reading once more, with Dunaj's silky head resting on his knees. Looking at the young lad with such an intelligent look, one could almost believe he, too, was impatient to know more about Jesus. At the end of an hour Palko was so engrossed with what he had been reading that he forgot even the presence of his dog.

The disciples worshipped at Jesus' feet; he had declared that he would be with them always, even unto the end of the world; that all power had been given unto him in heaven and on earth, and their duty was to go forth and teach men to keep and obey those things which he had spoken unto them!

Jesus was alive! Jesus was raised from the dead! And Jesus was now with him. Palko, clasping his hands together, prayed earnestly: "Jesus, Son of God, seeing that you have power in heaven and on earth, you see me, even though I may not be able to see you. I wish to tell you how much I love you, yes, much more even than I love my grandfather, and I wish to obey you. Help me to find the way to the true Sunshine Country."

Palko returned home that night earlier than usual, with a quantity of strawberries. He lighted the fire and prepared the stew for his grandfather, forgetting altogether that he himself had eaten nothing all day but a few strawberries. He was more than content with the great joy that flooded his soul. It seemed to him that Jesus had entered the little hut with him, and that now they were friends.

"See now!" he said, speaking to his invisible friend. "I am making the stew for my grandfather. Now I must go to the spring for water; the only thing I ask is that you will not go away before I return. I love you so!"

But strangely enough, it appeared to him that Jesus went with him to the spring.

Soon all was ready, and Palko anxiously waited for his grandfather's return, because, at last, he was going to tell his secret.

Eventually, Martin having gone to the city, Juriga arrived alone, a bit worse for drink, and in a bad humour. He rebuked Palko at every turn, refused to taste the stew, and threw himself, holiday clothes and all, on the bed. When Palko said timidly that he would crush his best clothes, Juriga gave him such a slap on the face that the boy hurried out of the hut with a red cheek, which stung for quite a while.

"Don't count it against him, Lord Jesus," said Palko, "because he does not know that you are here."

When Juriga was at last asleep, Palko without fear ate the stew, now almost cold, and, in spite of the fact that he had forgotten the salt, he was so hungry that it tasted delicious.

"You will truly return again in the morning, Lord Jesus," said Palko. "I am so tired now I'm nearly asleep already, but I do not want you to go away."

The First Beams of Light

Late on the following day Juriga awoke with a headache. When he opened his eyes the first thing he saw was the light of the hearth fire, with Palko seated at one side, his legs crossed, and one arm around Dunaj's neck. The ruddy curls of the boy mingled with the dog's soft white hair. Both of them seemed to watch the fire with equal pleasure as it merrily sparkled and crackled away. The whole scene was such an enchanting picture that the old man's heart was softened. He remembered how he had struck Palko the night before, and for what reason? What ill had the little fellow done?

"Why did I get drunk? I didn't drink very much, but somehow it went to my heard. It's lucky that Martin isn't here today. Yet, if he hadn't gone away yesterday, I would have returned home as soon as we came out of church; but, being alone, I yielded to temptation as soon as they called me!" Juriga, heavy-hearted, scratched his head; he would have given anything to have avoided an interview with Palko that morning, being greatly ashamed of himself. What would old Rasga have said if he knew that, on his return home drunk, he had struck and sworn at the lad whom he had committed to his care?

But it was necessary to get it over somehow, so he spoke.

"Search in my cape, Palko, and you will find a little package for you. It's something they gave me at the marriage feast last night."

Jumping up, Palko greeted his grandfather heartily, and was soon busy untying knots in an old handkerchief. What treasures were there — sweetmeats of all kinds, candies, cinnamon buns and cakes!

"Is all this for me, Grandfather?" he asked, sinking his teeth in a bun.

"It's all yours, my son; seeing the way you were treated last night, it's little enough. With this cursed drink, one doesn't know what one is doing. At first I tried not to take a drop, but what can you do when all the others press you?"

"Look, Grandfather," said the boy, "that you struck me last night is nothing. What I am frightened of is that he will go away from here. He has already heard you swear, and I doubt if he can remain where men get drunk."

The old man stared at Palko, bewildered, not understanding to whom the boy referred.

"Are you speaking of Martin? He's not here, and he won't be free for the rest of the week. I know he doesn't like drunkenness."

After washing, Juriga seated himself at the table.

"No, I am not speaking of Uncle Martin," said Palko.

"Have you ever seen a book that describes the country where the sun never goes down?"

"No, son, I've never read a book like that; who told you about such a book?"

"Oh, but there is, and it also tells a lot about Jesus!"

And Palko began to tell his grandfather how Jesus was born and how a terrible man tried to kill him, and what he began to do after his return from a far country.

"But, my boy, you are telling me the Gospel story of Jesus Christ! You seem to know more of the story than I do in spite of my age. How have you come to know all this?" said the astonished old man. Palko started to tell Juriga how it all happened, but just then Liska the woodcutter entered, and they had to stop. Juriga and Liska went out to start on a new group of trees, but when they were some distance away Palko came running after them.

"What do you want?" asked Juriga.

"I pray you, dear Grandfather," and the boy's great eyes reminded the old man of the blue mountain lake nearby, when the sun shone upon it, "I pray you do not drink anymore. I'm so afraid that Jesus may not stay with us if you continue to drink or swear."

"Let me alone!" cried the old man, angrily.

But Palko was convinced that his grandfather would drink no more, and as the days lengthened into weeks, the other workers on the mountain began to say one to another: "What has come over Juriga? He goes no more to the tavern."

Time passed without the opportunity for which Palko longed, namely, to tell his grandfather how he had come upon his great 'find'. Juriga was so busy cutting trees and preparing the proper wood for the carving and shaping. On returning to the hut at night he just ate the supper, which his grandson had prepared for him, and then dropped on his couch to sleep, too tired for any conversation.

Martin did not return until Saturday, and to Palko he seemed particularly depressed. Palko longed to ask him the cause of his sadness. He remembered his own state of mind the night he cried so bitterly on learning of the death of the Lord Jesus, but as Martin hardly ever took any notice of him Palko felt it would be too forward of him to ask about his private affairs.

Heart Searchings

During the following week Palko found no time to visit his Sunshine Valley. His grandfather had promised the people at the chapel house, as well as the shopkeeper of the village, that his grandson would bring them strawberries and mushrooms every day. The task of filling his two baskets each day, and carrying them down the mountain, took up a good part of his time.

Visitors had arrived at the chapel house. They were Father Malina's sister, her husband and her two children. Every time Palko arrived with his baskets the cook gave him a piece of meat or cake or fine white bread; and one day, when he arrived just at lunch-time, he was taken in and given such a meal as he had never tasted in his life before. The old cook noticed that he set aside a portion of the meat to take to his grandfather, and so she added another big slice. Dunaj, Martin's dog, who had become almost like a shadow to the little boy, and who had come in for his share of these good things, had eaten so much that he panted heavily as they climbed the mountain path, homeward bound. Juriga was greatly pleased in opening his surprise parcel to find that Palko had thought of his grandfather.

"You may be sure that I shall remember your kindness to me, Palko," said the old gentleman, as he counted out the strawberry money. "I will put this money aside for you. Just keep on gathering fruit while you can, and when winter comes, and footwear is needed, we will buy shoes with your earnings."

So Palko worked hard at his gathering and did good business in the village, especially with his two principal customers, the shopkeeper and the chapel house. Nevertheless, he would have gladly done without all the titbits that came to him through these friends in the village, if he could only have gone more often to the cave to read the sacred pages, which would tell more of the wonderful story of God's Son, and the way to the true Sunshine Country.

If the Valley were not so far away, or if he could have carried the book home with him, he would have saved so much time. However, the book was not his, and, therefore, what right had he to carry it home? Thus he always hailed with joy the arrival of Sunday, which gave him more time to visit the cave and learn more of the contents of the precious volume. One day he had found a spot that was just covered with the finest strawberries and had gathered a basketful, while Dunaj made life miserable for the lizards and rabbits of the mountainside.

"But why," said Palko, still thinking of his last reading, "is the same story repeated four times in the book? I suppose it might be to make people pay more attention to it." Besides, there were new details here and there in each account, such as that of the story in the gospels of the paralytic man who was lowered by his friends through the flat roof of the house to the feet of Jesus that he might heal him, and how strange it seemed to the people who stood around that Jesus should tell the man his sins were pardoned.

What were his sins? Yesterday, Father Malina had explained sternly to his nephews in Palko's presence that it was indeed a great sin to steal fruit from the neighbours. Perhaps the paralytic had been robbing an orchard, too, and had fallen out of a tree; who knows but perhaps that was the cause of his awful sickness? That being the case, why was Jesus the one who forgave him? Perhaps he was the owner of the orchard. "But if I do a wrong thing, is it necessary for Jesus to pardon me? That must be so, for the book says he has the power to forgive sins."

Interrupting his work among the strawberries for a moment, Palko put his hands together and bowing his head, said: "I have sinned so many times, and until now I have never asked anyone for pardon. Lord Jesus, seeing that you have the power to do so, I pray you please pardon me, too." After waiting a little while, he resumed his work and said: "Many thanks, for I truly believe you have pardoned me in spite of all the wicked things I have done. I had no idea before how bad I have been. Have I not broken my grandfather's cane so that he might not beat me any more? Also, did I not steal my uncle's whip, and eggs from my aunt? To be sure, they both punished me well for it, but I must confess that what I did was wicked. I wonder what Jesus meant when he said: 'Those that are well need no physician,' and 'I have not come to call the righteous, but sinners to repentance.' What does it mean — repentance? The people that came to Jesus showed their repentance by confessing their sins. I suppose that each one would tell wrong things that he had done, and then Jesus pardoned him. So then, everybody in the world ought to tell everything to Jesus in order that he might pardon them. I suppose everybody does do so. Only I, poor ignorant boy that I am, I never knew anything of this, because I am still so small. I'm going to ask grandfather this very day if Jesus has pardoned his sins."

Soon Palko had filled his two baskets with strawberries and picked a good quantity of mushrooms.

"Come here, Dunaj, we must go at once! Leave the little birds in peace. Who knows but that it is sinful to frighten them as you are doing? Poor little things, see how terrified they are as they fly away. If I had to frighten them so, I suppose it would be sinful of me, but being only a dog, he would excuse you."

Little moved by his sermon, Dunaj trotted contentedly behind his master. As they came out of the wood, with the village lying before them at the foot of the mountains, Liska caught up with them.

"Hallo, there! Where are you off to so early?"

"I am taking these strawberries to the chapel house, Uncle."

"Go ahead, my lad; you will soon have earned those shoes of yours."

"And you, dear Uncle, where are you going?"

"I? I am going to confess. It is a long time since I have done so. But I suppose it is necessary to fix up my sins once in a while."

"You are right," said Palko, and the boy's great blue eyes sparkled with joy, "and so you too have settled the question of your sins. I suppose you have told the Lord Jesus of the wrong you have done, and he has pardoned you as he did the paralytic man?"

"What are you talking about?" said the astonished Liska. "I only said I was going to confession."

"What is it, then—to confess?"

"Oh, I go to church and Father Malina gives me absolution and he forgives me my sins."

"Father Malina! Has he the power to do that?"

"What a funny boy! How do I know? I only know

I'm a sinner, and it's better to come to the priest to confess two or three times a year, and I expect God will be good to me."

"So, then, you don't know for a certainty that he has the power? When you come out of the church after confession, will you be sure that your sins are pardoned?"

"Nobody can be sure of that before one's death. When we die, we shall know all about that sort of thing."

"Uncle, if you go to Jesus, he will surely pardon your sins, just as he did the paralytic who was let down by cords before him through the roof of the house."

"What's that you say? Are you talking about Jesus Christ? But, my dear boy, we're just a bunch of poor ignorant people and the priest is like the Lord God on earth. He arranged everything for us. All I have to do is go to him."

"Then, has God said about him also: 'This is my Beloved Son, obey ye him'?"

"What on earth has happened to you, Palko, that you try to turn me upside-down with such questions?"

"Don't be angry with me, Uncle," and Palko's great eyes seemed to look right through those of the man beside him. "It's only that when I asked the Lord Jesus today to pardon my sins, he did it right away! If only you could know how happy I feel! Now, goodbye, Uncle, for I must go first to the lower village."

For some minutes Liska watched the retreating figure of the boy. "What is this he says? Christ pardoned his sins? What sins? I doubt if the dear boy has committed any. Oh, that I might also have the same certainty of pardon that he seems to have! But a man like me, who has committed so many more and done such terrible things! Who can be sure of pardon? We go and confess because all our forefathers have done so before us, and it must be the proper thing to do. Now Palko comes to question me as to whether the priest has the necessary power to pardon and to give absolution. Has not his reverence so affirmed it before the altar? 'I-as-the-servant-of-God-declare-to-you-by-virtue-of-my-sacred-office-that-your-sins-are-pardoned-you.' It is thus clear that he has the right — at least, by order of the church. It is as it should be and one might as well believe that which ought to be, so why trouble one's brains with the boy's questions?" Liska straightened himself and made his way to the village church, which was already filling with the faithful, who had come with the same purpose as himself, but not knowing much more than he did on the subject.

Meanwhile, Palko had arrived at the chapel house and, finding the door open at the end of the garden, he saved both time and steps by taking a short cut to the kitchen door. It so happened that he met Father Malina coming down the garden walk. He was too young a man to have so much grey hair, and such a wrinkled and pallid face.

Palko kissed the hand of the revered father, as his grandfather had told him was the proper thing to do.

"Well, well, and so here come the strawberries again! I suppose you gathered them last night," and his reverence selected a couple of the most luscious ones. "No, indeed, sire," said Palko, "for then they would not be fresh by now. I gathered them this very morning, so I had to be out in the field before sunrise."

"Well, you certainly ought to come to something, my son, seeing you are not afraid of work. Take these over to the kitchen and tell them I would like you to have a good dinner. Better leave your dog here, for he'll be likely to have trouble with the cat."

That day everything seemed to be wonderful for Palko. In the first place, he had found such a lot of fine strawberries that morning, and then Father Malina had been so kind to him. Lastly, in the kitchen they had given him such a dinner that he wouldn't need to eat any more that day, and, besides, they had filled his bag with buns and cakes and sweetmeats from some feast of the night before; and all this without forgetting to pay him a good price for his strawberries.

"Just wait a bit longer, Dunaj," Palko said on joining his dog again. "As soon as we get back to the mountainside you're going to have such a wonderful dinner."

Father Malina was waiting at the bottom of the lane.

"Well, my son, did you get your dinner?" he asked.

"Yes, sir, and I wish to thank you so much."

"Did they pay you? Show me what they gave you. Oh, my! Isn't that quite a lot for a few strawberries?"

Frightened by such a question, the boy stole an anxious glance at the priest to see whether he was serious, but it was impossible to read anything in that impassive face.

"I really don't know," said Palko, somewhat abashed, "Grandfather told me to ask that much, but besides the strawberries there were quite a few mushrooms, sir."

"Then, this is your grandfather's money?"

"Oh, no, sir, it's my own. Grandfather puts it aside to buy shoes and fur linings for me for the winter. What a wonderful thing it will be if I am able to earn enough money to buy a new shirt, but I'm afraid they're too expensive." (Palko longed to have one of those finely embroidered shirts, with wide sleeves, that were an essential part of the national dress in Czechoslovakia).

"That's true," replied Father Malina gravely. "Here is something to help you to obtain the necessary sum more quickly," and a few silver pieces slipped into Palko's pocket to keep company with the copper ones already there. "Also, as you constantly bring us fruit from the mountain-side, I would like to have you try some of our fruit from the garden here." Saying this, he put a couple of big pears into Palko's hands. How his mouth watered when his teeth went into the luscious side of one of them, but the other one went into the bag for his grandfather. Then, politely thanking his benefactor, he turned to go, but suddenly changing his mind, he came back again.

"What's the trouble, my son?" said the priest kindly. "Did you forget something?"

"No, sir. You are the priest of the church, is it not so? The people come to confess to you. Is it true that you have the power to forgive their sins?"

At this unexpected question, Father Malina was somewhat taken aback.

"Have you something you wish to confess to me, my son?"

"I? Oh, no, sir," and the boy's eyes sparkled.

"What do you think I did? It was just what the people did by the river Jordan. I, too, confessed everything to Jesus, and he has pardoned me, I'm sure of it! I only asked you because of the others, and I want also to know more about the whole thing, sir. Perhaps they do not know that Jesus is willing to forgive them all their sins, if they would only come to him. Are you also able to forgive them?" and Palko's tone was earnest, "Has God said of you, also: This is my beloved Son, obey him'?"

Putting his hand on the ruffled brown hair of the lad who looked up at him so earnestly, the priest gave him a keen look. A great friend of all the people, he had a special love for children, often saying that the future of the nation was with them. In this poor boy, the son of a humble woodcutter, he saw at once a great soul.

"No, my son, our Lord has not spoken of me in that way; that would have been impossible, because Jesus Christ is the only begotten Son of God. Him we must hear, and him only. The only thing I am able to do is to assure the people that the good Lord will pardon their sins, if they are ready to do many good works."

"Then a priest cannot arrange everything like God can for the people?"

"Certainly not! Who has told you such an absurd thing?"

"My Uncle Liska told me so. As for you, sire, surely the Lord will pardon you also, if you ask him, because you do so many good things such as the good dinner you gave me today, and the money for my shirt. I am sure that you obey God and his Son Jesus."

"There goes the bell, Palko, I must hurry along."

The priest went into church waving a friendly hand to the little boy, who turned up the mountain path accompanied by Dunaj.

"I am sure that you obey God and his Son Jesus!" As he performed his priestly office these words continually came back to Father Malina and seemed to pierce his very soul. "That which this lad has spoken of has been the life-long problem of my heart. In spite of all the good that I do to others, I know I do not obey thee, Son of God! I know my sins are not pardoned, and that these unhappy ones who come to confess today shall not find either the real peace or the true pardon. Yet, being the parish priest, it is my duty to receive their confession. But where has this boy found such absolute security and confidence that he can say: 'I confessed everything to Jesus and he has pardoned me, I am sure of it'?"

Engrossed in his thoughts, Father Malina took his little devotional book, which happened to open at that passage in St Matthew where the angel said to Joseph: "And thou shalt call his name Jesus, for he shall save his people from their sins." These words took possession of him with such power that he almost forgot his waiting parishioners.

"Redemption, liberation from the power and guilt of sin. I can't achieve this! Jesus Christ has brought it to the world, but how must I go to him?"

Meanwhile, as Father Malina, with an agitated heart and an afflicted spirit, officiated in the little village church, Palko had climbed to his cave and was soon lost in his reading. A storm was gathering at the other end of the valley and the thunder muttered behind the clouds, but in the Sunshine Valley all was yet peace, and warmth, and quietness, as Palko, oblivious of his surroundings, wandered in the new land of the Scriptures that had so completely captivated him.

A man was climbing up the mountain path looking toward the ground. It was Martin. He strode along quickly seeking shelter from the threatening rain, and giving little heed to the lovely valley spread before him. The sadness on his face today seemed darker than that which was now obscuring the horizon.

It was on such a day as this, he thought, that, some years before, he had committed an act which he never could undo, and which never could be driven from his memory. By day it pursued him at his work, and by night it kept him from sleeping. Now, as he strode along the mountain looking for some protection, the sound of the thunder found an echo in the thunder in his own soul.

Great drops of rain began to fall, and Martin looked all around trying to discover a hiding-place in order to save his good clothes from the rain. Happily, about twenty yards distant, he saw a rock and running to it he found the entrance to the cave, inside which an interesting picture presented itself. There, seated on the ground, with one arm around the sleeping Dunaj, was Palko, absorbed in reading a book which was propped up on a rocky support. Martin didn't care much for the boy, the sight of whom always seemed to send a stab of pain through his heart. The reason was that years ago, he, too had possessed a son whom he had lost through that terrible act of his, and the bitter tears he had shed through the long years since had not brought back that priceless treasure to him. At this moment, looking in at the peaceful scene before him, he could not help thinking, "My little Mischko would be about the same age now." With a sore heart he hid his face in his hands. Somehow, he wanted to press young Palko to his heart.

At that moment a flash of lightning, accompanied by a loud clap of thunder, awakened Dunaj, who, raising his head and cocking his ears, rushed to his real master with a yelp of delight, wagging his tail contentedly.

"Uncle Martin!" exclaimed Palko, springing to his feet. "However did you find the way here?"

When the storm roars, one does not like to find oneself alone. So it was that Palko forgot his natural shyness in Martin's presence.

"I just came in here to find shelter from the storm. How do you come to be here?" It was the first time Martin had ever spoken in a friendly manner to the boy.

"I will tell you all about it, Uncle Martin, but first come in where it is dry and sit down. Here is a table and chair for you, too."

"This seems for all the world like a dwelling," remarked Martin, "but you haven't told me yet what you are doing here. Your grandfather thinks you are off gathering strawberries and mushrooms."

"I finished my work and returned from the village long ago," said Palko.

"But have you had anything to eat?"

"Yes! They gave us a wonderful dinner at the chapel house, didn't they, Dunaj?"

The dog enthusiastically gave assent to this remark by licking his chops and giving a wag of his tail.

"Well, but it is now four o'clock in the afternoon. Why do you stay here all day, instead of going back to the hut?"

"I have not had time. You see, it is Sunday, and grandfather, therefore, does not need me so I want to hurry to get to the end of this wonderful book. My! What thunder! I remember some time ago storms like this made me terribly afraid, but now I know that the Lord Jesus is always with me, I'm not a bit afraid when it thunders. Be quiet, Dunaj! It's just as if the good Lord himself was speaking to us."

Martin could not keep his eyes off Palko. What a lovely child! How was it that he had not paid much attention to him until this moment?

"What is this book you have here? A New Testament! Where did you get it from? Haven't you got one at home?"

"No, but I will tell you all about it from the beginning, if you want me to."

"All right! I'm listening," said Martin, seating himself with his legs doubled under him on the floor of the cave with Dunaj at his side. Palko told his story, and Martin listened now with a lively interest, while the boy explained to him how he had discovered the Sunshine Valley and the Holy book at the same time, and how he was now seeking the road that led to the true Country of the Eternal Sunshine.

Opening the book at the first page, Martin studied, as well as he could in the gloom, the words of good counsel written there.

"What have you read today, Palko?" he asked the boy.

"Oh, a good bit, up to the place where it tells about the terrible time when they tortured him until he died. I suppose further on it will tell about his resurrection as in the other part. I wished to finish the part called St. Mark."

"Well, as soon as the clouds pass by and I can see clearly enough, I will read you the rest, it ought not to be very much," said Martin.

It seemed as if the sun had heard his words, for almost immediately a ray of light shot through the clouds, although the rain continued to fall quite heavily.

"All right, Palko, here comes the light, let's sit down and read." So with Martin on one side of the opening of the cave and Palko on the other, with Dunaj in the middle, the reading began. At their feet lay the beautiful Sunshine Valley, now made even more lovely by the refreshing rain; above their heads the lightning still crackled; and in the west the sun seemed to sparkle with a new splendour, while far away in the east a wonderful rainbow seemed to arch over the door of heaven itself. The rain gradually ceased, and all about on the grass blades the raindrops shone like a million diamonds, as far as the eye could see.

Martin read about that wonderful Easter morning, when the three women, on coming to the tomb, found the great stone door rolled away, the sepulchre empty, and the angel who gave them the glorious message: "The Crucified One lives and waits for you in Galilee!" He also read how the risen Lord appeared first to Mary Magdalene, and sent her to the disciples, and afterwards to the two wayfarers on the road to Emmaus; and finally to the eleven whom he rebuked on account of their unbelief, to whom he gave the final order to go into all the world and preach the gospel. Then, oh, then! Martin read in the closing words to the astonished boy something which he had not yet heard, namely, that Jesus suddenly ascended up to heaven where he seated himself at the right hand of the Father.

Palko looked up into the sky. Now he knew where Jesus had gone, and why, although living, he was no longer on earth. He was there above and beyond that beautiful door in the sky. The Father had a glorious throne up yonder and the Son was seated at his side.

"Now I understand!" he exclaimed in a tone of triumph. "Up there, on the other side of that beautiful door is where one can find the true country where the sun never goes down! What we are looking at here is only the outer border. Is it not so, Uncle?"

Martin did not answer; perhaps the boy was right. God's Word was not unknown to him as he had been the best scholar in the school, and he had had the highest mark in the catechism class. He had known where the Lord had gone, only he had never thought about it before. Christ had always appeared somewhat vague and strange to him (as he is to so many thousands of those who have been brought up in the knowledge of the gospel story, who know all the details but have never really considered the Saviour as an actual living person, one who would become a reality in their own lives).

"Oh!" sighed Palko, "if I could only reach the end of the book quicker, but it is important that I should read line after line, and word after word. It goes so slowly, yet I daren't miss anything, as I do not know on what page it might tell me something of the road to the Sunshine Country.

"I am the Way, the Truth, and the Life." Martin remembered the words and slowly recited them out loud.

"Yes," said Palko. "I saw those words on one of the pages further on, but I did not understand what they meant. Would it be that he will come to show me the way to the Country, and take me by the hand and lead me there, so that I will make no mistake?"

"That is quite possible; but just now he is very, very far away from us up there. Haven't we just read about it here in the book?" At Martin's words, Palko lifted his eyes in dismay to that beautiful door again. Yes, it did seem far, so very far away. Here he was a poor boy down on the earth; what a great distance it seemed to where Jesus was in heaven.

"Don't worry, Uncle Martin," said Palko suddenly, with a new look of joy on his face. "He is not only up yonder, but have I not read in the other part his promise to the disciples: 'Lo, I am with you always, even unto the end of the world'? His home, yes, it is above, but he lives near to us, and at this moment he is here with us."

"With us! Where?" said Martin, incredulously.

"Oh, Uncle Martin, please do not speak so," said Palko softly. "You will offend him. Haven't you just read to me how 'he rebuked them because of their unbelief!' I think it must be something like that with Jesus. He is here but it's just that he has made it so that we can't see him with our eyes. It's like he's invisible perhaps? He can do everything—and so I believe that he is here." A clap of thunder sounded in the distance like a solemn "Amen!" to Palko's last words.

"Shall we read on in order to get to the end of the book more quickly?" asked Martin.

"Yes please, Uncle. You read so well and so clearly that I understand every word."

One, two and three hours passed, without their having noticed the length of time, and, when at last Martin closed the book, the rain had ceased some time before, and the paths were now completely dry.

Palko's surprise had increased more and more as the reading progressed. What beautiful stories there were in St. Luke, which he had not found in the previous parts: the birth of John the Baptist, and some wonderful new things about the Lord Jesus and his childhood; the appearance of the angels to the shepherds in the country and, later, how the shepherds found Jesus in a manger in the town; and then afterwards how the boy Jesus visited Jerusalem with his parents. Palko almost wept for joy, it was such a beautiful story. "I never thought that Jesus was once a boy like me!" exclaimed Palko, "and he, no doubt, would be very obedient and win everybody's love."

Martin seemed to catch Palko's enthusiasm. It was as if he were reading these things for the first time, and they truly rejoiced his heart.

"Why leave the book so far up here?" he said as they were starting for home, "Let us take it with us and read a few pages each day. Your grandfather can then profit by the reading also. On Sundays you can carry it with you, and when the book is finished we can leave it here again."

Palko gladly agreed to this arrangement.

"I have never dared to take it away before," he said, as he went home with Martin, "but if you think the Saviour will not think ill of us for taking the book away, it would be splendid to have it with us."

It was late when at last they arrived at the hut, but, as Palko was with Martin, his grandfather did not scold him. Supper was soon ready, and the old man was delighted at the sight of so much money and the magnificent pear, which Palko had brought home for him.

That night Palko dreamed of a beautiful boy who beckoned to him, saying: "Follow me, I am going to lead you to the true Sunshine Country." After ascending behind his young guide to the crest of a rugged mountain crag, he was able to make out a group of three crosses, and as his friend pointed to the centre one he saw the form of a Man nailed there. Palko began to cry and sob so badly that Martin, who was lying near him, thought it better to wake him up. "What's the matter, son, what are you crying about?"

"Uncle mine! I cannot bear to think of it! What terrible suffering they must have caused him!"

"He's still dreaming," said Martin to himself.

"Jesus, my dear Jesus," said Palko quietly, "how could they be so cruel as to make you suffer so? If it is possible to do so, please explain to me why your heavenly Father did not save you, especially when he loved you so."

Palko had long since fallen asleep again, but Martin still lay awake with Palko's last words ringing in his ears. Yes, why did Christ have to suffer and die and why did God forsake him? Finally, he remembered the words on that first page of the boy's New Testament: 'Read with attention, line after line, and it will teach thee the way.' Could it possibly give him an answer to those terrible questions which came to trouble his own lonely and unhappy soul?

***

Every day from that time onwards, after mid-day meal, which had previously been their siesta, they all read together a portion from the Holy book.

Juriga listened admiringly to Martin reading. Why, the man read quite as well, if not better, than the schoolmaster! He spoke to neighbour Liska of the book discovered by Palko, and especially regarding the strange paragraph on the first page. This aroused Liska's curiosity and from that day onward Liska also became one of the group of daily listeners in Juriga's hut. They were old truths and stories that they had known for many years — at least some of them were — but as the reading progressed the whole of it seemed new, and of infinite value. If someone had given them a New Testament in the ordinary way, probably they would not have been at all interested, but the strange mystery that surrounded the finding of it as well as the living and beautiful faith of Palko, seemed to urge them to believe in a new and vivid way also; and so at the end of the day's work Liska and Juriga would get together and talk over what they had heard at the midday reading.

"Look, friend Juriga," said Liska one day, "ever since that boy of yours asked me whether the reverend Father in the village had the right to pardon my sins, I have not ceased to think about the matter. There's not a shadow of doubt that, although we are only simple villagers, he cannot be in place of God for us—that much even I can understand. Well, I know also that my sins are not pardoned and that I am not reconciled to God, and I cannot but wonder what use it is my going to confession."

"Perhaps," said his friend, "we may discover from the book the real truth," and Juriga leaned his shaggy head on his hand, with a thoughtful air. A little later he said: "When Martin read to us the other day about the paralytic, I would have liked to have been that same man, and to have been carried to Jesus to be pardoned in the same way. I would go to the end of the world to find him."

One day, after the usual reading, Palko said to Juriga: "Grandfather, the corner where I sleep – may I consider it my own house?"

"Of course," answered his grandfather, "you can call it your palace if you like."

"Many thanks, sir," said the little boy, apparently well-satisfied with the reply. That night when Juriga and Martin returned from work they gazed with surprise at the transformation which Palko had made in his place. The whole corner had been swept absolutely clean, the bed placed in perfect order, and a large pitcher, although badly nicked around its top, was full of freshly gathered flowers while the wall was draped with leafy branches, as in the time of the Easter feast.

"Well, I declare!" said Martin, "you must be expecting a distinguished guest, Palko."

"Yes, indeed, Uncle. He has come to stay with us, and I have received him into my house as Martha and Mary did!"

Palko's elders smiled at this reply, but the boy's little corner was such a sharp contrast to the disorder that reigned in the rest of the hut that the two men began to fix up their part, and Palko was given orders to sweep out the whole house.

In the Sunshine Valley

"I wonder where Palko is?" and as he spoke, Juriga peered across the clearing in front of the hut.

"Palko?" and Martin seemed to come out of an unpleasant dream, to judge by his face, but it cleared immediately on hearing the boy's name. "I saw him going up the mountain road a little while ago with the book under his arm, and Dunaj was following him. I imagine he was bound for his Sunshine Valley."

"Just at present," said Juriga, "I don't believe he thinks of anything else outside the Sacred Scriptures. It's amazing the way he seems to take it in."

"It's certainly true," agreed Martin, with his chin on his hands. "He's like the child Jesus used for an example to his disciples. He believes every word in the book."

"Don't you think we do the same?" asked the old man. "No, Uncle," replied Martin, with a shake of the head, "our life would be very different from what it is if we believed the book as he does. For instance, do you believe with all your heart that your sins are pardoned through Jesus Christ?"

"As to that," said Juriga, clearing his throat a bit to give himself time to reply, "I am certainly a bit hazy in my mind. Our God is very, very holy, and I am a terrible sinner – that much has become clear to me ever since you and Palko brought the book home to this house. Another thing I know, and that is, that the boy is certainly changed. He, at any rate, believes that his sins are forgiven."

"Yes, said Martin, "and I really believe his sins are actually forgiven."

"And yours, my son?" and Juriga was all ears for his answer.

"I —" and Martin's head went down once more; "there's no chance of that for me — when I — when I consider —" and poor Martin could say no more.

Juriga knew there was something weighing on Martin's mind, which he longed to get rid of, but felt that it was ground that he himself had better not tread upon, so he did not pursue the subject for the present.

***

Meantime, Palko had climbed the hillside to the valley on the other side, but today, instead of entering the cave, he sat down in the field nearby with his back against a great rock. At the same time he carried on his usual conversation with Dunaj and with the birds.

"Look, Dunaj, why do you trample on the flowers and dig them up like that; they certainly weren't planted for you to destroy. And the birds, why do you always love to frighten them away? Another day I'll not take you with me at all."

"Come here," he said to a chaffinch, which rather timidly came hopping along quite near to them. "You see, Dunaj isn't really very bad, only a bit foolish, and besides, he doesn't know what a sinner he is, because he's only a dog." The chaffinch didn't have the confidence he should, perhaps, have had in Palko's statement, for he thought it wiser to remove himself to the branch of a neighbouring tree. "Now you must leave me alone," said Palko in a general way to all the birds, butterflies, beetles, and principally to his dog, "for I must get on with my reading."

No prince could have wished for a lovelier seat than the one Palko had at that moment. It was a rock beautifully covered with thick moss of the colour of an emerald and surrounded with a frame of wild roses, whose pale pink blossoms formed a shade on both sides, while his back was supported by another mossy rock of varied shades. In front of him lay the magnificent Valley of Sunshine.

On that day something happened to Palko that has happened to many others as well when reading a very exciting book. Their patience becomes exhausted, and they take a peep at the last page.

"Now that we are all reading the book together," he said by way of excusing himself, and at the same time burying his elbow in the moss with his chin in his hand, "I just wish to get a good look at the end." Opening the book at the last page, he began to read:

"And he shewed me a pure river of water of life, clear as crystal, proceeding out of the throne of God and of the Lamb.

In the midst of the street of it, and on either side of the river, was there the tree of life, which bare twelve manner of fruits, and yielded her fruit every month: and the leaves of the tree were for the healing of the nations.

And there shall be no more curse: but the throne of God and of the Lamb shall be in it; and his servants shall serve him:

And they shall see his face; and his Name shall be in their foreheads."

"How beautiful!" said Palko, "this must be the real Sunshine Country at last. I feel it away deep down in my heart. With that magnificent river that flows from the Throne of God and of the Lamb. One thing I would like to know — what Lamb it is that has a throne in heaven." He raised his eyes to the sky above him.

"The Lamb? I know: 'Behold, the Lamb of God!' it was the name given to Jesus by John the Baptist. And the trees along the river are always bearing fruit the whole year round. I wonder what that means. 'There shall be no more curses.' One thing's certain: there won't be anybody there that uses bad language."

After reaching this wise conclusion he added: "I must tell our neighbours, the woodcutters in the huts around, that they should not swear any more. It's bad enough to give the Lord Jesus offence when he hears them down here, but it's certain that they won't be allowed to do so up there. Then it speaks of the servants around the Lamb's throne. My, wouldn't I like to be one of them? If only he would accept me as one of them! But then," he pondered, "often I have difficulty in getting up in the morning to carry water for Grandfather and then, when I ought to get the firewood, I play around with Dunaj instead. When Grandfather Rasga said good-bye to me for the last time, I remember he said: 'My little son you must work hard for Grandfather Juriga; and do everything he says.'" Putting his hands together and closing his eyes, Palko said: "Lord Jesus, I pray you pardon me for not helping my grandfather better. I wish to work for him more faithfully from this day on, in order to prepare myself to be one of your servants when we shall come to the true Sunshine Country. How I should like to be near your throne right now!"

Then, renewing his reading: "And they shall see his face; and his Name shall be in their foreheads." "Well, then!" and Palko again nodded to the smiling valley beneath him. "Wouldn't I like to have his Name written on my forehead? That would be a great honour for a poor, foolish boy like me."

Palko had not noticed that he had raised his voice; and that someone had come round the corner of the great rock and had stood listening. He, therefore, jumped on hearing a voice say: "Why do you call yourself a poor foolish boy, Palko?"

Then he stood up quickly in surprise at seeing Father Malina in his Sunshine Valley.

"How do you come to be here, sir?"

"Did you think, Palko, that the mountain was all yours, and that I had no right to breathe a little air outside of my garden?"

"No, sir!" said Palko, flushing. "I would not say or think such a thing, but it is so far away, and this is Sunday. Who will be preaching the sermon to the people in the church?"

"My, what an inquisition! Well, you see, I preached this morning, and now, on the doctor's orders, I have come to spend a few days here, for I am not very well."

"Here? On the mountain? And where do you live?"

"In the house of the forest guard."

"Oh, that's quite near! But please do not be angry with me if I ask you one question," and the boy seated himself at the priest's feet, as he had already taken a seat on the rock. "Who told you about the Sunshine Valley?"

"The Sunshine Valley! Is that the name of this place?"

"Yes, sir! That is to say, I don't know," said Palko, a bit puzzled. "You see, one day I saw over there the door of heaven and, just beyond it, the place where the sun never goes down, so I thought this must be Sunshine Valley on the border of the Sunshine Country."

"Oh! So this is where you find the door of heaven!" and Father Malina looked around with renewed interest at the snow-capped crags, the great forest and the valley far below. "The fact is that one seems to breathe the air of heaven here. But, my little son, where did you get the name Sunshine Country? Had you heard before of some such place?"

"With your permission, sir," and Palko's eyes sparkled, "I'll tell you all about it."

"All right, go ahead," said his Reverence.

Comfortably seated on the moss, Father Malina listened to the boy's story of his quest for the Sunshine Country where the sun never goes down; how he had found this lovely valley, and at the same time the wonderful book which had made plain to him so many things concerning the real country of the eternal sunshine. How in the day of the great storm he had seen what seemed to him the very door of heaven opening when the rainbow shone out on the other side of the valley, hanging high above the mountain pass with its seven magnificent colours. Unconscious of the tears that began to well up in the priest's eyes, Palko told of his reading of the day, and how he had asked the Lord Jesus to take him into his service.

"Let me see the book," said the priest. After looking through it, he said: "Would you mind leaving it here in the cave? Then, I could also come from time to time and read it as you do 'line after line,' to seek with you the road to the true country of the Sunshine that has no need of the sun or of the moon—for the Lamb is the Light thereof."

Palko thought for a moment while a struggle took place in his heart — then he straightened himself. "All right," he said. "Uncle Martin leaves us tomorrow, and I do not read well enough to make it very interesting for the others. I can come up here and read for myself, and if you happen to be here at the same time you can read it to me — can you not, sir?"

"Good! That's splendid," said Father Malina, "and if you wish, we can read some of it now. But, before we begin, just show me this marvellous cave you've been talking about." So up they got and with Palko leading the way, the priest followed, not without difficulty, to the cave's mouth.

"This is indeed lovely," said Father Malina, really surprised and delighted. "You are certainly right! It really appears to be a dwelling. Here is something better than a seat — it seems more like a couch. And the lovely flowers you have brought! I can see you, too, love beautiful things!"

Palko's guest looked, with evident pleasure, at Palko's well-swept palace with its flowers and ferns.

"Well, you see, sir, the Lord Jesus has promised to live with me, and I thought he would be better pleased if I made the place beautiful and tidy."

"Do you believe that he is always with you everywhere, Palko?" The priest's tone was very different from that of Uncle Martin or his grandfather, so Palko readily replied to the question: "Oh, yes, sir I'm sure he's with me always and is here."

"The simplicity of a child's faith," murmured the priest with a sigh, as he seated himself and, with his elbows on the table, he remained for some minutes without moving, as if in prayer.

Not wanting to interrupt him, Palko remembered that nearby he had left hidden between two rocks some lovely raspberries, which he had set aside for his grandfather. He thought, however, that his grandfather would be delighted when he heard who had reaped the benefit of his find. He had no dinner plates, but there was a tree quite close that had large broad leaves that would serve well as plates. He soon filled these with the luscious fruit, having washed them carefully in the brook which ran through the rocks at one side. This done, Palko came back to the cave, full of happiness at the thought of bringing such a royal gift to his honoured guest.

As Father Malina was busy reading the book, Palko laid his gift at his guest's side. The priest raised his head and his pale face lit up with pleasure at the sight of such rare fruit. "Are these for me?" he asked in surprise.

"Yes, sir," said Palko. "Please do me the favour of taking them. How many times have you given me such lovely meals at your house, and now, what a pleasure it is for me to give you something." The boy's face shone with happiness as the priest began to eat the berries with enjoyment. At the same time he took from his pocket some fine white bread, a rare sight for Palko, which he shared with the boy, and Dunaj also.

"Now I have promised to read to you," he said, "so sit down, for I see there is little time left this afternoon. Will you be coming tomorrow?"

"I'm afraid not, sir," said Palko, "for I shall have to help Uncle Martin with his baggage, as he leaves us."

"In that case, I shall take the book with me and bring it back here to you the next day, either in the morning or in the afternoon."

So Father Malina read aloud for a while of how Jesus went up to heaven, how the angels announced his return to the earth some day, and how the Holy Spirit came down upon the disciples.

"Will you please tell me, sir," said Palko, as they came out of the cave, "What is the Holy Spirit?"

"He is the Spirit of our Lord Jesus Christ, and the third Person of the Trinity," said the priest quietly. "Every Christian should have the Spirit, because it is written in this book: If a man have not the Spirit of Christ, he is none of his'."

"Of course, sir, you have the Spirit," and the pure innocent gaze of the boy was fixed on the priest's face—"for you surely are his?"

To any other person than Palko, Father Malina would have had little difficulty in replying. Had he not been baptised? Did he not belong to the Catholic Church, the only dispenser of Salvation that he knew of? Had there not been placed upon him the unction of the priesthood?

"Before I answer your question, Palko, I wish to consult this book in order to give you an answer you will understand."

For a little while they walked in silence.

"What are you thinking about, Palko?" asked the priest.

"What must I do, sir, so that the Lord Jesus may give me the Holy Sprit?" said Palko, taking the priest's hand.

"Well, it's written in the book that the heavenly Father will give the Spirit to those who ask him."

"Then," said Palko, "do you mean to say that the Spirit can enter my heart?"

"Without a doubt, my boy; look at the sun! See how it marches on, immense, radiant, and majestic in its path through the sky. Now see this little drop of water on the blade of grass. If you look closely at it what do you see?"

"Oh!" exclaimed Palko. "Why it's the sun inside it!"

"Yes! Now, my Palko, good-bye until the day after tomorrow."

Martin Speaks of his Past

Next day Martin went down the mountainside carrying a heavy bundle, accompanied by Palko with a smaller one. As the sun rose at the valley's end, he turned to the little boy.

"Palko," he said, "the other day you said your sins were pardoned; how do you know that?"

"Because I have confessed my sins to the Lord Jesus, and he has taken them all away, I asked him to and he has done it."

Martin looked wistfully at the boy as he said: "That's something I cannot, no, and never will be able to say."

"Why, Uncle, how can you say that? Jesus said he has power to forgive sins, and he is so kind he will do the same for you as he has done for me."

Martin shook his head. "No, not me. He cannot pardon me. Listen, Palko, I will tell you now what I have told no one else here. I'm telling you only that you may pray for me, so it will be a secret between us.

"Some years ago I had a happy home with my beautiful young wife and our little one, a boy of twenty months. Gradually, however, I began to drink heavily and often came home in a disgraceful condition. One day I entered the house in this state, and seeing only our little boy playing in the front parlour — he had only just began to toddle about — I took him for a walk. My wife, who was sleeping in the next room, was informed by a neighbour when she awakened that I had been seen about an hour before heading for the path to the forest, taking our son with me. On returning late that night, I was alone! Where I had been, God alone knows!"

Overcome by emotion it was some minutes before Martin could proceed with this story. "Frantically my wife questioned me as to the whereabouts of our boy, but I could only shake my head stupidly at her. When I came to myself, my wife was nowhere to be seen. We found her at last on the mountainside calling wildly the name of our little son. Oh, how we searched for him, for I had not the least idea where I had been, nor where the poor little lad had wandered. Weeks and weeks went by, and still we searched nook and cranny and precipice, fearful sometimes of what we might find at the base of a rocky chasm, but it was all in vain. At last the strain became too great for my poor wife, and her reason gave way. Oh, it was terrible to see her in such a state, so young and so beautiful. At times she is quite well, and then, suddenly putting a shawl over her head, she will rush from the house to disappear up the mountainside calling for her little one. I can only quiet her by going with her until, completely exhausted, she is willing to be led home again. How many times have I seen her walking vacantly from one side of the room to the other trying to arrange the little empty cradle, which still stands in its accustomed corner after all these years!

"Never, never, shall I touch a drop of the accursed drink again, but how shall my vow of abstinence bring us back our boy? When we were reading the other day the story of the poor man possessed with devils whom Jesus healed, I could not help thinking of how the drink demon had taken hold of me and had gradually brought me to ruin, and my family as well. No! No! Palko, there is no pardon for me!"

"Oh, poor Uncle Martin! Don't say that!" exclaimed Palko. "Let us ask God to give you back your son, and also that he may pardon your sin and heal your dear wife. I'm sure he will do it!"

Martin only shook his head, and then turned to Palko, saying: "What do you want me to bring you when I come back?"

"Well," said Palko quickly, "I should like a copybook and a pencil."

"All right, you shall have them, for all your kindnesses to me. Your grandfather has given me your money to buy a new suit, and I shall add to that a hat and shoes for the school next winter."

"A new hat!" Palko cried. "That will be wonderful, for I've worn this one so long that it's almost falling to pieces. I have been such an expense to my poor grandfather, I hope I may be able to pay him back some day."

"That should not be necessary if you are his grandson; he should be glad to have a lad like you," and Martin's eyes rested tenderly on the boy.

"Oh, but he is not my grandfather! He has but taken care of me. My own grandfather was Rasga, who died two years ago. We came here together, but he was ill and had to go away. He left me in the care of Juriga, but I call him Grandfather just the same."

"So you are an orphan? Well, why not come with me for a while? Here comes Liska. He can tell Juriga that I've taken you with me for a little holiday."

Palko's eyes shone at such an offer. To go to the city, with its great shops and other wonderful sights that he had heard about. But suddenly, shaking his head, he said, "What would the Lord Jesus say if I left my grandfather that way? Who would bring the water, cook the soup, and sweep the hut? No, Uncle

Martin, let us leave it to the will of God. Only come back quickly, for we shall miss you very, very much."

And as they parted, Martin murmured to himself: "And how I, too, shall miss the lad."

Palko helps Father Malina

"It's strange," said Liska, the next day, to Juriga, "Martin is different from the rest of us. He hardly said a word the whole way along the road, as I helped him carry his things. He acts as if he carried a heavy burden on his mind."

Juriga had noticed the same thing many times, but he only said:

"We're going to miss him, nevertheless; may God restore joy to him, and bring him back soon to us."

Indeed, Juriga was not mistaken; the hut seemed empty, for even Palko was not there. The forest guard had come with a message from Father Malina asking for the boy's services.

"You must indeed let Palko go, Father Malina will pay you well in return," said the forest guard.

Juriga wondered what Palko would think of the arrangement, but when the lad found that his grandfather would be amply provided for in his absence, he jumped for joy.

"Oh, the Lord is so good! I told Martin we should leave it to God's will, and just see what he has done for me," he said to the bewildered Juriga.

Never had Palko's simple heart dreamed of a life like the one which now began for him. He slept on a couch in the same room as the forest guard, and how very comfortable it was. Palko, used to his bed of straw in the corner of Juriga's hut, never imagined there could be anything more comfortable than that couch. On rising in the morning what breakfasts they got, prepared by the skilful hands of the forest guard's good wife, and what sweetmeats she tucked in his pockets when he set forth as a guide to Father Malina. Morning after morning he led him through shady glens and across brooks, or for a climb over the rocks. That good man did not complain. He gathered flowers, plants, and mosses and was very grateful for his young guide, who showed him the most lovely views of all the mountainside. There could be no better guide than Palko who knew every nook and cranny and stone for miles around. When they were tired and stopped to rest, Palko, who carried the priest's travelling cape, was ready to cover him with it. The little boy found his companion an expert in the names of the plants, flowers and birds. All this the priest taught Palko, as well as giving him lessons in reading, writing and arithmetic.

At times, the priest, who was not over strong, would lie down and sleep for a little. During this time, Palko would take the opportunity to look for strawberries, as he did not wish to return to the house without taking some offering to the good lady who was so kind to him. Happily Dunaj had not accompanied his master. "I leave him to you, Palko," Martin had said before leaving. "I'm afraid he would miss you too much if I took him with me." Thus Dunaj was always present on these happy outings, for where Palko went, there Dunaj went also.

For Palko the happiest moments were when the priest took the New Testament from his great pocket to read to him. To tell the truth, though, there were times when he heard many things too difficult to understand. He was tremendously interested in the story of the apostles and all their wonderful doings. After the book of Acts had been gone through came a letter entitled, 'To the Romans.' This time Palko could hardly understand any of it, while the priest, on the contrary, could scarcely get on quickly enough with the reading, going back time after time to it, and meditating thereon, especially when he came to these words: 'God commendeth his love toward us, in that, while we were yet sinners, Christ died for us.'

"Sir!" cried Palko, "how glad I am to hear this; it sounds so good to me!"

"You are right, my son. God gave us his all. Christ died for us!"

"He died for us?" said the astonished Palko. "That's strange! I thought he had died because wicked people had crucified him. How, then, did he die for us? And why?" Palko was greatly interested.

Opening at the Gospel of St. John, the priest read from the third chapter about Moses and the serpent, and then told the story of the Israelites and what happened to them after they had left Egypt. They had rebelled against God, and had done wicked things. Poisonous serpents had come forth throughout the great camp and had bitten them and many were dying, but at God's command, Moses placed a brazen serpent on a pole, and as many as looked on the serpent in faith were healed. "That story," said Father Malina, "is to teach us about our sins, and the brazen serpent, by which they were saved, shows us how Jesus Christ became accursed for us, and was put on the Cross for our sins."

As Palko seemed to have difficulty in understanding this, the priest went on to tell him of the sufferings of the children of Israel in Egypt. He told him how Moses was sent by God to deliver them from their slavery under Pharaoh, who refused to let them go, and how the Lord, after performing many miracles by the hand of Moses, finally sent his destroying Angel in judgment upon Egypt. How God protected the Israelites by ordering them to kill a young male lamb without any defect on him for each family, and put his blood on the side posts and lintel of the door of each Israelite dwelling, in order that the destroying Angel, seeing the blood of the lamb put there by the family, might pass over the house without destroying any of that family. The priest solemnly repeated the words: "Christ our Passover is sacrificed for us. Behold the Lamb of God which taketh away the sin of the world!' Do you understand, Palko? We also should have perished because of our many, many sins, but, God commendeth his love toward us, in that, 'while we were yet sinners, Christ died for us.' He suffered death in our place and so he is the Lamb (the Passover Lamb) of God that taketh away the sin of the world."

Palko suddenly hid his face in his hands. He had forgotten his friend; he was oblivious to everything but one thing, and throwing himself face down on the grass, he sobbed aloud: "Lord Jesus," he cried, "my beloved Lord Jesus! Now I understand why the heavenly Father did not answer when you cried, 'Why hast thou forsaken me?' it was because you had to die for our sins, as the lamb died in place of those Jews. Now, now I see why you and you only, have the power to forgive our sin, our wicked sins, that were the cause of your death!"

When Palko rose from the ground he found himself alone, and in the place where Father Malina had been sitting, he found the book still lying open at the third chapter of John.

From that day, the priest seemed more than ever absorbed in his meditations, and in prayer. Sometimes in the middle of the night Palko would wake to find a light burning in the priest's room, and he would softly steal over to the door to find his friend on his knees.

On Saturday, at the end of the second week, Palko heard the wife of the forest guard say to her husband: "Instead of getting better, he seems to be getting worse. I'm sure his poor face gets paler every day. He seems, too, to have something on his mind, something that's troubling him greatly. I overhead him say the other day, as I passed his door: 'If I only knew, if I only knew — can it be that — that we —' but he never finished the sentence, so I don't know what he was talking about, although I'll admit I'm dying to know. He says he's going to the village to preach tomorrow, but to my mind he'd be better off here in the house."

"Look here, my dear!" said her husband; "he would no more be able to go without preaching than I would without my gun, or you without your flat iron. There are others, I know, who wouldn't trouble their heads much if they missed a few Sundays' preaching, but he is too conscientious for that."

When they went into the forest that morning, Palko said: "Is it true, sir that there is something troubling you?"

"Who told you that, my son?"

"Something was said in the forest guard's house that made me think so, sir," said Palko humbly, "and the good wife there is worried at seeing you so pale and sickly too."

"Don't misunderstand, Palko, I am sick, but there's no cure for this kind of sickness."

"Not even by the power of the Lord Jesus?" said Palko, terrified, taking the pale hand of the priest in his brown ones.

"Well, of course, he would be able to cure anything, but —"

"Then all we need to do is pray! Don't you remember that Jesus healed all that came to him, even the paralytic, who hadn't even asked for healing for himself? Shall we just pray and ask him now?"

"Are you going to help me pray?" said the priest, astonished.

"Of course, just as the messenger of the Centurion did, saying to Jesus that 'he is worthy for whom he should do this'."

"But, please do not pray like that, for I am not worthy."

"Well, how shall I pray? Perhaps it would be better to pray like the publican who stood afar off by the temple door, and who was looked on with disdain by the other man who admired himself so much?"

"Yes, you are right, Palko, the prayer of the publican indeed is the only one that I can say."

The priest spoke no more and returned earlier than usual to the house.

In the afternoon Palko was ready to accompany his new master to the chapel house to spend the night there, but something seemed to trouble him.

He confided his troubles to the good wife of the house, while she was washing up the dinner dishes. "How can I go to the village with Father Malina in these clothes? Oh, if I had my new suit and hat here now, and my new shoes!" Palko was quite upset.

"Now, don't you worry, Palko mine, I've thought of all that. I've got a suit that used to be my son's, which I think will fit you. That will be a present for having helped Father Malina so faithfully, and for your kindness in running so many errands for me." Saying this, she produced a lovely snow-white shirt, a pair of blue trousers, and the boy's own little jacket, which she had cleaned with such surprising results that Palko hardly knew it. Neither could he recognize himself that afternoon, when he stooped to see his little figure reflected in the pool of the brook close to the house. He polished the priest's shoes and also his own, which had new laces that the good lady had given him as well. His heart was overflowing with happiness as they started for the village, and even the priest caught some of Palko's joy.

"May God bless and keep you, and a million thanks, Ma'am," Palko cried back to his hostess as they turned the bend in the path.

"Let us take the same short cuts that you and Dunaj take when you come with strawberries to the chapel house," said the priest.

"Oh, no!" said Palko. "That would hardly do; for the forest guard warned me not to take you by unsafe paths."

The priest laughed. "If he could only have seen the slippery impossible places I have had to climb over on our mountain walks in order to keep up with you two. Don't be alarmed, I'll not betray you; I've had too good a time for that. Besides, it was in the most difficult places that we found the loveliest flowers. Now, before we arrive at the village, tell me something about your family."

More than content to see his friend so cheerful, Palko hastened to tell him how, two years before, he had been brought by his grandfather, Rasga, to these mountains, and how the poor man, finding himself very ill, had returned to town to die, there, leaving his small grandson in the hand of his old friend Juriga.

Father Malina listened with great interest to this story. "If your grandfather, Juriga, should die, what would you do, and where would you go?"

Palko stopped and looked with great astonishment

at the priest. "I suppose the Lord Jesus would come to my help, just as he did when Grandfather Rasga died. The hut on the mountainside will not be ours if Juriga should die, and the little house in the village – I will show it to you as we pass by – is owned by his sons, so that I could not stay there. Perhaps I could find someone who would take me into their service. If you, perhaps, sir, should need a strong man about the house at that time, I would certainly like to be the one you choose."

"That's a good idea, Palko," and the priest's eyes twinkled. "In case your Grandfather Juriga dies before I do, you must come and stay with me and with no one else. Promise me now."

Happy at such an arrangement for the future, Palko put his sunburnt hand into Father Malina's delicate thin one as a sign of the pact.

The conversation was interrupted by the arrival of some of Father Malina's parishioners, who accompanied them to the door of the chapel house, where Palko was given a most excellent supper and a hot bath before he went to bed. He was so sleepy he could hardly say his prayers, and was soon in the land of dreams.

Awaking next morning at daybreak, Palko slid out of bed, and was putting on his clothes quietly so as not to disturb Father Malina, who had his bedroom adjoining his, when he saw his friend seated by the window in the next room with the New Testament on his lap. He was not reading, however, for his eyes were closed, a smile was on his face as if in the ecstasy of some delicious dream, and his face, usually so pale, was lit up as if the splendours of a sunrise had touched it.

The little boy slipped away noiselessly to wash himself at the well in the courtyard. After drying himself and combing his hair carefully, he stole back on tiptoe into the room. Still seated by the window, the priest had now opened his eyes and was reading softly to himself. Palko heard the words pronounced distinctly as his friend read aloud: "For by grace are ye saved through faith; and not of yourselves: it is the gift of God: not of works, lest any man should boast. For we are his workmanship, created in Christ Jesus unto good works, which God hath before ordained that we should walk in them." Then he saw his friend turn some pages and, after a short pause, heard him read the following: "Not of works of righteousness which we have done, but according to his mercy he saved us, by the washing of regeneration, and renewing of the Holy Ghost."

Palko came in quietly and seated himself on the stool at the priest's feet.

"Good morning, sir."

"Palko," said his friend, passing his hand through the little lad's hair, "it is indeed a good morning for me, the best morning I have ever known, like the one when Mary saw her risen Lord in the garden by the empty tomb."

"So you are not sad any longer, sir?" questioned the boy.

"No, my son, on the contrary, I am happy, very happy! And I can tell you why, for you and you only will understand me, and rejoice with me, for I have found this night the road to your Sunshine Country, and can at last give you a clear answer to a question you once put to me. Yes, I have received the Holy Spirit; I, too, have received the Lord into my house as Martha did, and as the drop of dew we saw on the mountain received the sun. For the Sun of Righteousness has come to dwell with me with healing in his wings. Now, Palko, just thank the Lord with me that he has pardoned all my sins, too. I have not slept all night, but it has been the most wonderful night of my life!"

After they had prayed together, Palko said: "Father, you must rest a bit or you will not be able to preach your sermon today."

"My sermon!" said the priest, as he tenderly kissed Palko. "I shall preach today as I never had before! Now I shall speak as a true witness, for, like Saint Paul, I have seen the Lord in the way and the scales have dropped from my eyes. While for years like Saul of Tarsus, I blindly served an unknown God, I can now say: 'I know whom I have believed,' and like the man who was born blind, and whom the Lord Jesus healed and gave him sight, 'One thing I know, whereas I was blind, now I see'."

But, as Palko insisted and brought him a cushion, he lay down on the sofa, and his little attendant covered him up with a heavy shawl.

As soon as his master was asleep, Palko left the room. He was just about to leave the house without breakfast, for he wanted to climb the hill to see his grandfather that morning, but the old serving maid spied him and would not let him go until he had swallowed a generous supply of milk and carried off with him a large piece of delicious white bread.

He hurried up the hill, for he had not seen Juriga except once or twice in the passing in the last two weeks. "I have certainly missed you," his grandfather had said to him but, never mind, you must do your duty to his Reverence, who knows what good may come of it some day."

Paths they have not known

Meantime, the unexpected had happened in the little hut on the mountainside. Juriga had received a letter, not from his sons in America, but from Martin, who had written as follows: "I have found that my wife is at present in a fair state of health; but my mother insists that I ought not to leave her in the future, and I feel that my mother is right. At the same time I must return immediately to the mountain, as you know, or I shall lose considerable money. I, therefore, intend to bring my dear wife with me, and I believe that Palko's company will do her good. He is such a fine lad, it will make her happy to be with him. I would pay well for the use of a portion of the hut. My wife is a good cook, even though, at times, she suffers so when her head is bad. With Palko near it will be as if the Lord has sent his angel to help take care of her. As I read yesterday these words in Isaiah: 'and a little child shall lead them,' I seemed to see Palko before me. At any rate, is he not the one who has brought you and me into the light? Truly then, perhaps he will be the one to lead my wife out of darkness too." Liska, who read the letter to Juriga, had to stop more than once to wipe his eyes, for Martin had told him of the mental state of his poor wife, while Liska, in turn, could not help but tell Juriga something of the story also.

To Juriga it was a great pleasure indeed to do what little service he could for Martin. There was plenty of room in the hut, and it could be divided off. Let the poor woman come, and perhaps, in God's mercy, Palko would be a great blessing to her.

Little did Palko dream what news awaited him on the mountainside. The very last thing that could have entered his head was that he would not be allowed to return to help his beloved friend. But, when Monday morning arrived, Juriga flatly refused to let him go back to the village. Martin was to arrive with his wife that very afternoon, and Palko would have to help care for her, especially while Martin and Juriga were busy on the mountain. He would remain behind in the hut with her, or she could go with him when he went to look for strawberries.

No matter how Palko tried to make his grandfather understand that Father Malina could not do without him, it was useless.

"Leave me in peace — you and your priest!" at last exclaimed the exasperated Juriga. "At most he's only a foreigner, while Martin is one of us, and it is our duty to help him first. Listen, you go about saying the Saviour is with you and hears all that you say. I don't know what he will be thinking, if you will do nothing to help a poor man in his trouble, so say no more."

Palko took the water jug and started for the spring, but on arriving here he threw himself on the ground and cried as if his heart would break.

"Dear Lord," he said, "he's not a foreigner, and I did want to help him, for I love him with all my heart. Please, I want to go back to him." Then, suddenly, like a voice that spoke, there came to his mind a verse the priest had taught him one day from the Old Testament: 'I will bring the blind by a way that they know not; I will lead them in paths that they have not known; I will make darkness light before them, and crooked things straight. These things I will do unto them, and not forsake them.' Palko went back to the hut at peace again with all the world. He was still in the dark, but God seemed to have promised that he would make the darkness light before him.

"Grandfather," Palko said, "shall I have to give up my corner and sleep with you when Martin and his wife come?"

"I suppose you will," said grandfather.

"Then can we receive the Lord Jesus here in your corner?"

"Yes, of course," said the astonished old man. "Then I am content," said Palko happily.

It must be said, however, that, when he started out for the forest guard's house to ask him to take a message to the priest that he could no longer help him, he had a heavy heart under his small jacket, especially when he knew he could not even go and see his beloved master personally to tell him all about it.

What a pleasant surprise awaited him however: there stood Father Malina before the forest guard's house, and he had spied Palko coming up the path.

"Welcome, welcome, my son! I have risen even earlier than you this morning to go for a long walk with you."

"Oh, dear, I can go no more walks with you, sir!" and poor Palko burst into tears. "My grandfather," he sobbed, "has asked me to greet you in his name, and to tell you to look for someone else to take my place, as he needs me. He says a rich man like you will be able to find some other person."

"My money cannot bring me another Palko," said the priest, putting his arm about the boy. "Why does he need you so much? Perhaps he would let you come to me if I were to speak with him. Besides, I cannot stay here more than two or three days."

"Dear me, no! It would be no use!" sighed Palko.

Drying his tears he explained why he would be needed in the hut, and added how sorry he was to leave his friend's service.

"Now," he said, "I wish to obey my grandfather, but at the same time I am wondering whether the Lord Jesus will be angry."

Father Malina seated himself on a fallen tree trunk, and Palko knelt at his side.

"Angry," he said, "surely not. But I suppose he will be quite surprised."

"Surprised at what?" said Palko.

"Let us see," said Father Malina. "Did you not offer yourself for his service but a few days ago? He has taken you at your word and has accepted you as one of his young servants. If you were in my service you would go without question wherever I sent you, and do whatever I ordered you to do."

"Oh!" cried Palko, "how willingly would I do whatever you ordered me to do, and so much more whatever he should ask."

"Well, then! He is the one that orders you now, and I can hear him say: 'Take up thy cross and follow me'! Do you not believe that Jesus would have preferred to stay with his disciples whom he loved so well? But when his Father said to him: 'Take up this heavy cross on thy whip-mangled, bleeding shoulders, and carry it to Golgotha, and let them nail thee to it there.' What did he do? He obeyed!"

"Then you believe, sir," said the boy, flushing, "that the Lord Jesus is asking me to leave your service and to go to work for Uncle Martin and his poor wife? Will that be my cross?"

"I am sure of it, my son. It is your duty to obey and accept the task cheerfully. God knows why he puts this poor soul in your path of duty, just the same as he knew what he was doing when he sent you to me," and the priest saw the lad through eyes that grew a bit dim.

"Then you think by working for Uncle Martin and his wife, I shall still be in his service?"

"Undoubtedly, Palko! And you shall surely be his messenger."

"Perhaps he will give me the privilege of finding their little boy," exclaimed Palko.

"Their little boy! What are you taking about?" asked the priest. "What little boy is that?"

"Oh, I forgot, I should not have spoken of it to anyone, for Martin told me not to mention it. It is a secret between us, but I will tell you this much, now that I have gone so far. Some years ago they lost their little son on the mountain, and never, never have they been able to find him, and Martin's poor wife—but oh! I must tell you no more, and please do not mention it to anyone, for Uncle Martin would be so angry."

The priest had heard something from Juriga one day that made him now turn and look at the boy eagerly. "How old are you, Palko?"

"Nine, sir."

"How many years ago was it that they lost their boy?"

"I'm not certain, but I think Uncle Martin said it was about seven or eight years ago."

"Have you told your grandfather anything of Martin's story?"

"No, sir, for Uncle Martin would not like me to. You see, I think he was a bit ashamed to let Grandfather Juriga know — that is — oh dear, I must not tell anymore please," and Palko's eyes filled with tears of distress and perplexity.

Father Malina's face had heightened colour as he gently said: "Never mind, my dear, dear boy. God's ways are past finding out. I am going to prophesy; I think that the Lord Jesus is going to give you the joy of finding that poor woman's child."

"Do you really think so? Oh how wonderful! Where do you think he is?" exclaimed Palko excitedly.

"I don't think he is very far away, Palko. Meantime, work well for your new friend, and the day will come, I believe when you will thank God for having been able to help her."

A strange and solemn feeling came over Palko. He remained silent a moment with his head in his hands, and then suddenly turning he said: "I certainly am very sad!"

"Sad! And why should you be sad now?"

"Because I should have known it was Jesus who called me, and I refused to serve him."

"Oh, Palko, the same thing happened to many older people. We begin by offering our services to the Lord and then, when he orders us to do something contrary to our own wishes, we refuse to submit, or to humble ourselves, forgetting that he has said: 'Let him deny himself, and follow me'! Don't let it trouble you, Palko. Just remember what you told me you had done before. You prayed and confessed your sin and he pardoned you, didn't he? Do it again, and then go and help Uncle Martin and your new aunt as faithfully as you have helped me."

Then the priest prayed for Palko, asking that he should be to Martin and his poor wife the child that should lead them to Jesus' feet as he had led others from darkness to the light. The priest's lips trembled as he prayed.

Saying good-bye to Palko, Father Malina continued, "Now, don't be troubled. We shall still be the best of friends, for are we not both in the service of the same Master? When you come down to the village, always be sure to visit me. Here's your Testament. You're going to need it more than ever now. I have my Bible with me always, and besides, I have ordered many other copies so that my people may know the truth." Saying this, he took from his pocket Palko's precious New Testament. Kissing it reverently, he gave it to the small owner with tears in his eyes, as he added: "Oh, that it may be to others what it has been to me!"

They returned together to the forest guard's house and greeted their friends there, who, however, showed their annoyance at Juriga's arrangement, but the priest intervened. "Oh, it's all right now," he said. "I am beginning to know all the mountain paths, and besides, I shall be here only two or three days more."

The forest guard gave Palko a whistle with which to call Dunaj and a bright new coin, and the good wife added so much food and goodies that Palko could hardly carry all the gifts.

"When you come this way, even though you bring nothing to sell, be sure to stop and see us," she said, to which Palko gladly agreed.

His friends went with him to the hut, for he wished to thank the old workman personally for lending Palko to him; and to leave his pay in Juriga's hand. That Palko loved the priest, his grandfather well knew, and the old man said to himself that Father Malina would no doubt put a little money in the boy's hand also, but he was mistaken in this, for Palko came to Juriga after Father Malina had left him and excitedly showed a large sum of money that his friend had given him.

Juriga opened the parcel, which Palko had brought from the forest guard's house. "Look, Palko, you have not worked for nothing indeed! The Lord bless that good woman who has thought of us with such kindness!"

"Don't you see, Grandfather," said the boy, proudly, "you do not need to do all the work? I am going to do my part."

"That's right, my son! With this money I shall be able to buy myself new shoes for the winter. I have thought and thought about it, not knowing where I should find the necessary money. Surely it is the truth we have read in your book: 'Seek ye first the kingdom of God, and his righteousness, and all these things shall be added unto you'. It is as if God himself had rained it down upon us, and now we shall lack for nothing in the winter. Besides, you have brought enough food from the forest guard's wife to last for a fortnight," and old Juriga's eyes filled with tears. "They are not vain words when the book tells us that 'God is love'!"

Martin's Wife

Juriga did not anticipate that life in the hut with Martin's poor wife would be exactly pleasant, but he was ready to help, and put up with whatever discomfort might be necessary to relieve Martin's already heavy burden. He had not the faintest idea that the result might be quite the opposite.

Martin and his wife arrived late at night, tired out and quite content to drink the hot soup Palko had prepared. After arranging the bed with its clean sheets and blankets and downy pillows, which they had brought with them, they were soon safely tucked away for the night.

It was not, therefore, until the following day that Juriga could begin to study Martin's wife. "Poor thing," said the old man to himself, full of pity, "so young, not more than twenty-seven years old at the most, and so beautiful and gentle in her ways." Soon, little by little, her very presence in the hut, instead of being a burden, became a joy and a blessing.

From that first morning the meals of the small household were changed. By noon the little lady had prepared a delicious soup, which was taken with great enjoyment by everybody, including Dunaj, who welcomed most noisily and joyously his master and mistress. Then came a delicious cake with some nuts, which the new arrivals had brought with them. When Martin produced the suit and the promised new hat and shoes his wife helped Palko to get into his new clothes. From the first, the woman and child seemed mutually attracted to one another. She remained almost silent in the presence of older people, but as soon as she found herself alone with Palko she chatted with perfect ease, her beautiful voice soft and melancholy, like a summer breeze blowing through the birches of the forest.

When Liska appeared there was another cake for him to carry home, and his young hostess replied kindly to any question he asked. In fact, Liska had surreptitiously to wipe his eyes several times that afternoon, for he became quite overcome by emotion each time he looked at her.

"You have done right in bringing your wife, my son," said Juriga to Martin, by the end of the week. "You were not mistaken in thinking that she would be pleased with Palko's company."

"Who could resist the attraction that the boy holds?" said Martin, as he balanced his chair against the wall of the hut and gazed contentedly across the valley.

So it was that both Juriga and Martin could spend the whole day at work, secure in the knowledge that in such delightful company the poor little woman would not find the time hanging heavily on her hands. In fact, she herself found the time altogether too short for all the things she now seemed to find to do with Palko. In addition, she found many things in the little hut that required a thorough cleaning, including Palko's and Juriga's clothing and bedding. She cooked the meals, washed up the dishes, hulled and cleaned the strawberries, and prepared the other good things that she and Palko found in their long walks through the woods. When she had no other task to keep her busy, she would seat herself in the sunlit doorway to mend everybody's clothes and darn their socks. She even made a new shirt for Liska, who had no one to look after him.

Meantime, Palko surrounded her with every form of loving care. He told her the story of Sunshine Valley, to which he took her on the very next day after her arrival. He showed her his book, and explained to her something of its wonderful contents. She listened with great interest, even though at times she seemed to be somewhat lost in her own sad thoughts. Palko knew that at such times she was thinking of her own little one. He began to love her very much, a love that grew day by day.

One day, when his new auntie (as he began to call her fondly) was busy with some sewing, and lost in her own thoughts, Palko rested his curly head on her shoulder, saying: "It is so sad about your lost child, isn't it, Auntie? But don't worry about it. We are going to find him, you and I together. I have asked the Lord Jesus, and he is going to do it for me."

The woman suddenly jumped to her feet, looked at Palko fixedly for a minute, and then gathered him in her arms. Her cloak had fallen to the ground, and a ray of sunshine suddenly lit up both those fresh young faces, each framed in its locks of burnished gold and showing a most striking resemblance to the other.

"Do you believe that we shall find him, Palko?" she said finally, with an eager look on her face that Palko never forgot.

"I'm sure of it," Palko said, "for Jesus gives me what I ask of him. Tell me, what was he like?"

"He was quite like you, Palko, only, of course, he was quite small."

"Could he walk?" the boy asked, as he put an arm around his auntie.

"Indeed he could! When I took him by the hand he was able to walk quite a way with me, and he could take steps along by himself."

"What was his name?"

"Mischko."

"Mischko!" the boy repeated. "Well, then when we go to look for him, we shall call, 'Mischko! Mischko!'; or you had better do the calling, for my voice would, perhaps, frighten him, Auntie," and the boy's arm stole about her neck. "How long is it since you lost your Mischko?"

"How long?" She repeated, and her lovely eyes began to wander a bit. "Oh, I don't know, Palko! My head feels so strange. At times I can't remember anything at all, but I seem so much better since I came here to the mountain; somehow the weight seems to have been lifted from my heart."

"Do you know what you should do?" asked Palko. "Just live here with us always. In the winter we shall go down to the village, where we have such a big house and there would be plenty of room. There is a large living-room and a kitchen, and a little bedroom for you and Uncle Martin, and we shall all be so happy together!"

"I?" cried his poor auntie. "Nothing would please me better than to live with you always, Palko, dear!" and the tears welled up into Palko's eyes at these tender words.

"I do love you so much, I do indeed, Auntie, although to tell you the truth, at first I did not wish to see you come here, because it meant I should have to leave the service of Father Malina, whom I love, too, with all my heart. You see, he has taught me so many things, and I would so like to be with him. But he said it was my duty to come here because I was in the service of the Lord Jesus, and now I am so happy, too, to be here with you. But we were talking about your boy, weren't we?"

"Yes; and the people over in our part of the country are sure that a wild boar devoured him but I am not able to believe that," declared the unhappy mother, shaking her head. "I am certain that he is living, and we ought to find him. No, I don't believe he can be dead."

"Nor do I believe it, Auntie," said Palko. "All that the people say is just foolish talk. The Lord Jesus, whom I have asked to let us find him, would not have allowed the wild beasts to devour him. Perhaps somebody found your boy and has kept him safe all this time. So what would be the use of looking for him on the mountain? Who knows where he might be?"

Suddenly standing up and pressing her hands to her forehead, and with a fixed stare, the unhappy woman repeated, in a low voice: "Yes, who knows where he might be?"

"Never mind, dear Auntie," Palko said in a consoling tone. "Just remember one thing; the Lord Jesus knows. We will ask him to show us where he is. There are many women who come to the mountain, and we will ask each one of them if they have found a boy. Perhaps the Saviour will send us the one who has him safe in her home."

From that moment, whenever they were walking along together, Martin's wife would talk to Palko about her little Mischko. He in turn taught her to ask the Lord to show them where her son was, and she became quite comforted. Indeed, her pale cheeks became quite tanned, and she even seemed to lose some of her timidity in the presence of older people. She became a favourite with nearly everybody on the mountainside, and many tried to do what they could to give her pleasure.

Martin's joy knew no bounds. Before, his wife had behaved in a strained and unnatural way in his presence and endeavoured to avoid her husband whenever she could. Now all was changed. In the evening, when he sat down by the door of the hut, she would bring her knitting and sit by his side on the steps, with the look of the old tenderness in her eyes that he had known before Mischko disappeared. When they read aloud from the New Testament, which custom was resumed now that Martin had returned, she would sit close beside him and listen attentively.

Martin learned to believe in God's free and unbounded love for sinners, and at the same time to ask with faith in the Lord Jesus that he would heal his dear wife. Palko had repeated to them some of the clear explanations of the priest, and told how he had said that at last he had found the way to the true Sunshine Country through his reading of the book. Now Martin desired to find it also. He wanted with all his heart to have his poor wife find it too, but in her present mental state could she, by any chance, come to believe in the Lord Jesus also?

They read the book day after day, not only line after line, but also began again at the beginning, in order to pick up the forgotten threads. Every day they came to understand things better and better, and the way to the Sunshine Country seemed to open up before them all. Then there came a long spell of rain so this precious time was taken advantage of, and they progressed rapidly in their reading.

Liska also was found constantly with them, and did not return to his own house until after nightfall, making many an excuse to be with Palko, so that they might talk over together what had been read.

Father Malina is ill

Happy and pleasant though the life was that these five friends led together, Palko had the feeling that something was lacking. At times there came to him such a pressing desire to be with Father Malina that he would go down on his knees to pray to his Saviour; "Lord Jesus, I do wish to accept and bear my cross; but although I have not the whip-mangled shoulders that you had, still the cross is so heavy to bear! I do so want to be with my beloved friend."

Palko felt that none understood him like Father Malina, and so he longed to be off to the village for a visit to his dear friend; but no opportunity came his way for some time. The first Sunday the rain put an end to any thought of going, and the Sunday following, his grandfather had gone to church with Liska and Uncle Martin. When they returned in the afternoon, Palko asked permission to go to the forest guard's house to take the good wife there some strawberries, as an expression of gratitude for her wonderful gifts to them. Taking Dunaj with him, Palko started to run. He felt as if he had escaped from a cage, and Dunaj was delighted to find himself alone with his young companion.

"At last I shall be able to find out all the news about Father Malina." In Palko's happiness he made the hills echo with his shouts, while Dunaj also added to the noise. Very quickly they arrived at the forest guard's home. The good wife was alone in the house.

"A thousand remembrances from my grandfather,"

said Palko breathlessly, "and here are some strawberries and mushrooms with his compliments and thanks for all your kindness to us."

"My, my! What wonderful mushrooms! Where did you get them?" exclaimed the good wife. "Please thank him heartily for such a lovely gift, and such strawberries, too! They'll make a fine pie for my man today. Just sit down while I get you a cup of tea," and she bustled about and soon had a splendid feast spread out before Palko, such being her idea of a cup of tea for a hungry boy.

After a while Palko said: "If you please, ma'am, can you give me any news of Father Malina?"

"I think he's all right, except that there's been something so strange about him lately," and the good wife shook her head.

"Something strange about him, ma'am?"

"Yes! For the last two Sundays he has preached as never before." The good woman seemed to forget that she was talking with a mere child, because of the eagerness and attention that he gave to every word.

"That's it!" cried the boy, nodding his head with approval. "That's what he told me that last Sunday morning I saw him. He said he was going to preach as he had never preached before, for he had found the way to the land where the sun never goes down."

"He told you, that, did he? Well, that's what he said to us, for he used those very same words in his sermon. If you had not been with him day and night for two whole weeks, I would not speak of this to you, for you are so young, but he said that up until now he had not been a very good priest to us, because he had never been born again from above by God's Holy Spirit, and that he had had no assurance that his sins were all pardoned.

He also said that he had told us all he knew about the Lord Jesus, but that he had never really possessed him in his heart. Finally, he added that neither had we possessed him, but that he would teach us the way to him, because God had received him at last in grace, and had accepted him as one of his children. I can't tell it very well, for I'm only a poor woman, but I shall never forget that talk, nor the one he gave this morning. I could hardly wait for Sunday to come, so eager was I to know how he was going to show us the way. He has made us all see how good and holy God is and what great sinners we are, and that we should be lost for ever if we did not repent and come to God by faith in what his Son did, when he died on the cross for our sins.

"I can't tell you the impression he seemed to make, but it was so quiet in the church, you could have heard a pin drop, and one would have said that it was not Father Malina, who occupied the pulpit, but some other one, so magnificently did he preach. After the service we all remained in the churchyard, for we didn't seem to be able to move from the place; we were as astounded as if the Day of Judgment had already come of which he had spoken to us. And he told us about some book he had read whereby he found the way that leads to God and his Son, Jesus Christ, and he said that on the first page of the book was written something that I do not remember very clearly, but it was about reading it line after line."

"Here's the book," said Palko, "and here is what it says in the front of it!" He took from his pocket his precious treasure and read to her the opening lines.

"You have the book!" exclaimed the good wife, excitedly, taking it in her hands, "and how did you come by it, boy? Did Father Malina give it to you?"

"No," said Palko. "I was the one who loaned it to him." Then he had to tell again the story of his great find, which increased the good woman's surprise and delight. He told her how he and the priest had read the book together, and how together they had received the Lord Jesus, just as Martha and Mary had, and also the Holy Spirit, as the drop of dew received the sun.

"But, Palko, you talk like a saint, or like the Lord Jesus, when he was twelve years old, in the Temple," she said. "Would you mind lending me the book?"

Palko hesitated. "I would be glad to, but I have not read it through yet, and the book says, you remember: 'line after line'! To be sure, Uncle Martin has brought the whole Bible with him from the city, and we read from it every day, but I read from this alone, especially when I go to the Sunshine Valley on the hill up yonder, and when Auntie and I go out for a walk or to gather strawberries. I couldn't take the Bible with me, it is too big and heavy, and also it is quite difficult to find in the big book the stories and verses that I want."

The boy looked ahead of him, as if trying to find a solution to the problem.

"Now I have it!" he exclaimed suddenly. "Father Malina, when he returned the book, said that he was sending for other copies, so I suppose there must be many books like it in the world."

"Did he say that?" exclaimed the good wife joyously. "Listen, Palko, your grandfather won't be worried if you get back a little late today. I have some things here to send to Father Malina. Would you mind taking them for me, and ask him at the same time if he could let me have one of these books? I would be glad to pay him for it if the price is not beyond me."

"Good!" exclaimed Palko. "Now I've got my chance to see Father Malina."

Palko helped to pack the basket containing two wild pigeons neatly cleaned and dressed, the mushrooms he had just brought from home, a fine fresh sheep cheese, and some golden butter.

"Take it," said his hostess, "and give him my best regards. Tell him I shall never forget his sermon, and ask also that he will pray for me that I, too, may find the way that leads to God. Tell him I wish to do whatever may be expected of me, to make pilgrimages or pay masses, or anything else so long as I am not condemned for eternity."

These words started a train of thought in Palko's mind, as he started down the hill with his basket.

"What did she say? The Lord Jesus simply said: 'Come unto me,' and Martha and Mary never went on a pilgrimage before they received him into their house or paid for any masses. They just 'received' him, that's all I know. I'm sure the forest guard's wife doesn't know the story of the serpent of brass, or about the Israelites in Egypt who escaped death and punishment, because the lamb was killed for them and its blood put on their houses. You, Lord Jesus, are the Lamb of God who died for us upon the cross, that we, too, might not be brought to judgment for our sins! Why, didn't I tell her so? I will when I get back if I don't forget it. When she has the book she will understand it better, and besides, she has mine, which I've left with her in the meantime. She'll be reading some of it just now. What a shame that it doesn't tell all about this in the beginning. However, line after line, that's the way to come at the truth."

In next to no time Palko was at the chapel house. In the hall he met the old servant.

"Father Malina has been resting, and I would not let anybody disturb him," she said, "but he gave me orders never to send you away. Go in and show him what you have in the basket before taking it to the housekeeper."

Letting himself into the room quietly, Palko looked around for the priest, and finally, in the dim light, discovered him on the sofa. He had his eyes closed, but immediately opened them.

"Well, Palko, you are indeed welcome! At last you are here!" and the priest stretched out a thin hand. "I thought you were never coming, and I began to ask myself if you had forgotten me. There, now, don't look like that. I well know how you have wanted to come and see me."

"You can be sure of that," said poor Palko, trying hard to keep back the tears. Putting his basket on the table, and kneeling by the sofa he did a thing he had never done before. He kissed his friend tenderly on the cheek just as he would have kissed Martin's wife. This unexpected outburst of affection touched the heart of the lonely priest so much that he gathered little Palko in his arms and held him close.

"Why are you lying down at this time of day?" asked Palko, with great tenderness. "Are you tired or sick?"

"I am a bit tired, and also I have sharp pains that come in my side which make it difficult to breathe as soon as I start to walk. I have not spoken of this to anybody, and only tell you now that you might pray for me to the Saviour, and perhaps he might be pleased to heal me."

"Let us pray to him now, and then I will tell what I have come for. Lord Jesus, my beloved Lord Jesus, here we are with you, for you have promised to be with us, is it not so? I do ask you, please, to heal Father Malina. You know that he cannot preach when he's sick, and how necessary it is that he should teach the people the Way. The forest guard's wife wants to know all about it. Amen."

"Yes, Son of God," added the priest himself. "Thou who didst carry our infirmities, including mine. Thou knowest how much I would like to do for thee to help thy people who still walk in darkness. How many years have I been but a poor blind guide for these blind ones and I did not lead the sheep. Please let me repair the result of my blind carelessness. I did not know the Way or thy book and now this dear lad has brought me into the light, for thou has revealed unto babes what thou hast hidden from the wise and prudent. Now, Lord, I am so young yet, and have almost the whole of my life before me; if thou wilt heal me, I shall have but one desire, to be used in thy service. Amen."

A solemn silence reigned in the room, as in the church itself. Then Palko broke it exclaiming: "I believe, sir, that he will do what we have asked."

"Well, Palko, I believe he will let me complete my duty at least. Only I ask that you continue to pray for me. You know that we are both serving the same Master, and so we should help one another."

"You're feeling a bit better already, sir; are you not?" said Palko.

"Yes, I am better! As soon as you entered the room, I felt relieved. You see, Palko, no one has come to take your place, and on finding myself alone, and with this weight upon me, I have indeed been sore afflicted."

"You have no father or mother like me?"

"They died some time ago."

"But have you no grandfather or brothers or sisters?"

"I had them, but all my relatives have gone, except my sister, who was here with me a short time ago, but she could not stay, and lives a long way from here."

"Who, then, is the elderly lady that keeps house for you?"

"She is a distant relative of my father's. Just before your arrival I felt so lonely, I knew not what to do, but now the dear Lord has sent you to me, Blessed be his Name! What is in the basket you have brought?"

"Oh, I forgot. These things are from the forest guard's wife, and they will help to make you better. Just look! Wild pigeons," and Palko sighed. "Poor little things. It's a shame they had to die. Eggs. Then that special sheep cheese you're so fond of. And here's some lovely rye bread and just look at this butter!"

"Such a host of good things" and even the priest's eyes sparkled like Palko's, in spite of himself. "I have hardly eaten a mouthful today. I have preached twice, and held a funeral service, and done a few other things. Now I'm beginning to feel a bit hungry. There's a knife over there on the table. Cut a piece of bread for each of us, and we'll try the butter and cheese with it." Though the priest did not feel like eating much in the end he, nevertheless, urged Palko to eat plenty, and Dunaj, who lingered near the door, was not forgotten.

"There is one other thing I've forgotten, and that is the message from the forest guard's good wife to you. She said she could never forget your sermon, and also she wishes to buy a Bible if it does not cost too much. She said she wanted with all her heart to find the Way that leads to God, and if it's necessary to find him by making long pilgrimages, or paying for masses, she's willing to go to any length, only that she may find the way to God."

Palko had not thought that his message from the good woman would cause the priest so much joy. On hearing these words, he rose painfully from the couch, searched for a pile of shining new books arranged on a desk nearby, and taking one down, he exclaimed: "Blessed be God! I sent immediately for a good number, but I had no idea that I would need them so quickly." Seating himself at the table, he wrote on the first page the same words that had been found in Palko's book. Then, looking at Palko, he said: "So she wishes to make long pilgrimages and pay for many masses for her soul's sake if necessary? Tell her to read the words that I now write here. She'll find them also written in the book." And the priest began to write anew.

Palko looked over his shoulder, and this is what he read: 'For by grace are ye saved through faith; and that not of yourselves; it is the gift of God; not of works, lest any man should boast' (Ephesians 2:8-9). 'Not by works of righteousness which we have done, but according to his mercy he saved us, by the washing of regeneration, and renewing of the Holy Ghost... through Jesus Christ, our Saviour; that being justified by his grace, we should be made heirs according to the hope of eternal life' (Titus 3:5-7), for Christ hath redeemed us from the curse of the law, being made a curse for us' (Galatians 3:13).

At this moment the old housekeeper entered. "Here are some things for Palko and his grandfather," she said. "But, sir, how pale your face is! You should go to bed at once." Full of anxiety, she threw back the covers of the bed.

"Yes, yes, a little later, my dear. Just now I shall go with Palko a little way through the garden. We should not keep him longer, for he has a long road home."

Never had it cost Palko so much as it did now to leave his friend. "If you would but let me, I should prefer to stay with you until tomorrow at least," he said, when they were in the garden. "You are so lonely, dear sir."

"No, no, Palko, that cannot be! Your grandfather, who does not know where you are, would be greatly worried, and the forest guard's wife likewise. Go home now. I am much better, and I have the Lord with me. Tell your grandfather to come and see me tomorrow. I have something of great importance to tell him." Before taking leave of Palko the priest asked about Martin's wife, and if Palko was looking after her faithfully; but the telling of all this took some little time, so that the priest found himself at the foot of the mountain, where they sat down together to rest. So, when Palko finally arrived at the hut, he found his grandfather and Martin anxiously waiting, having gone out several times to look for him. He had had to go by the forest guard's house to deliver the Bible so that, although he had stopped there only long enough to change his baskets, and to see the happiness of the good wife on receiving the book, it was indeed late when, tired out, he tapped on Juriga's door. When he had explained all that had happened, they could not be angry with him, and Palko soon fell asleep in his chair by the fire.

"I wonder what the priest can want with me," grumbled Juriga, after Palko fell asleep. "What do you think it can be, Martin?" he asked. "Perhaps he wants to persuade you to return Palko," Martin replied as angrily as Juriga. "Gentlemen like him often have their fancies. Palko has told me that the priest made him promise to work for no one but him, if anything should happen to you. Perhaps he wants to ask you to give Palko to him now, for he would have difficulty in finding another like him. I pray you do nothing of the kind. The boy is no relation to me, but I could hardly bear to see him go. At times it seems as if I could not love a son of my own any more than I do that child."

"Don't be frightened," growled Juriga, clearing his throat a bit. "I'll not give him up, you may be sure of that. What would become of me without him? Is he not the one who has been leading me to God? Perhaps that may be the reward that Rasga said God would give me if I took care of him."

Martin would have liked more details regarding Juriga's relations with Palko, and his original grandfather, Rasga, but it was late, and so they all turned in for the night, and were soon lost in the land of dreams.

A Mystery is Solved

Early the following day Juriga was off to the village. Besides the visit to the priest, he had several other things to attend to at his house there, but, before doing anything else, he wanted to settle the matter with the priest, if it was what Martin thought.

He found the old servant crying at the door of the chapel house, and asked her what was wrong.

"Father Malina has passed such a bad night," was her reply.

"What? And my boy was visiting him only yesterday."

"Is Palko your boy? Father Malina thinks so much of him. Last night he went with Palko to the foot of the mountain, and when I met him on his return, he said that he expected you this morning, and told me to admit you at once. But frankly, I don't know that he is in any condition to see you today. The doctor has just left."

"What has happened to him so suddenly?"

"He has had a terrible sickness. His old aunt is in tears, and says it is a family infirmity, and that most of his brothers and sisters had died of the same thing."

Juriga waited in the servant's quarters until it was known whether he could see the sick man. At last the old servant returned to say that he could see her master, as the priest was very anxious to have an interview with Palko's grandfather, but that he should make his visit as short as possible.

"I wonder what he can want with me, especially as he is so sick," thought Juriga, as he drew near the priest's bed, and pressed the thin hand held out to him.

"I am glad you have come so quickly," said the sick man in a low voice, and Juriga could see that it was an effort for him to speak. "Did you not tell me one day that your friend Rasga was not Palko's real grandfather, but that his daughter had found him wandering on the mountains when a very little child? Now Palko tells me that Martin has a story that he could tell you, which I believe would clear up the mystery. Has Martin ever heard Palko's history as far as you know it?"

"No," said the astonished old man, "for I've told it to no one except you."

"Well, then," said the priest, "your duty is clear, Juriga. You must tell the whole story to Martin, and then I am sure that Palko will soon find his long-lost father and mother. Now, before you go — just one more request — I feel that I have but a few days more on this earth, for, as you see, I am a very sick man. Let Palko be with me for the few hours that remain to me in this life. He is such a friend to me and it is he who has led me to my Saviour. Yesterday, as soon as he entered the room, I felt comforted and strengthened. You will be able to have his company for a long time yet in health and life. I beg of you, let me once more have his companionship before I leave this world."

"I will send him at once," answered Juriga, struggling to restrain his tears. The old man seemed as one in a dream when he left the chapel house; as he passed through the streets of the village, he hardly noticed his neighbours. People remarked on his agitation and turned to look with surprise as he hurried up the mountain path. He seemed to see before him that pale noble face with its haggard, drawn features, and to hear constantly that soft voice saying: "Let me have his company once more."

"Just think," he said to himself as he climbed the mountain, "sick as he is, his first thought was not of himself, but of Martin and Palko, and of all of us! That was why he sent for me. He could hardly speak, but he summoned me to his bed of pain. And we—we have been denying him the boy. How is it that I have never told Martin Palko's story? Well, I must tell him without delay." Juriga could hardly wait until he got home. He found Martin alone near the hut. "Oh, Martin, what do you suppose Father Malina wanted?" Juriga's voice trembled as he spoke, "and we should remove our hats in speaking his name from this day."

"For one thing," said Martin, "I suppose he wanted Palko?"

"Martin, don't look like that! I found him very, very ill, for he had a terrible sickness in the night. He told me Palko was the one who had brought him to the Saviour, and that he wanted him near him."

"And you've agreed?" cried Martin harshly.

"Yes, my son, and I never go back on my word. We owe him infinite gratitude, and we can pay him but a small part of our great debt."

"Your great debt? A few miserable crowns you have received in just pay, and you call that a great debt!" and Martin sunk the hatchet he was using into a tree with all his strength.

"Leave your work, Martin, and sit down here. I want to ask you something," and Juriga eyed him so strangely that Martin obeyed at once, in spite of his anger. "What's the matter with you, Juriga?" he said, "that you look like that?"

"Tell me, Martin," said Juriga, "did you lose a boy once on the mountainside?"

"Did Palko tell you that?" said Martin.

"Palko has told me nothing. But is it a fact?"

"Yes," said Martin, "but how did you know?"

"I didn't know, I only surmised it from something that has just occurred at the chapel house. In what year and what time of the year did your boy disappear?"

Martin began to tremble at hearing Juriga's words, but he answered roughly: "Why ask such a question?"

"Oh, nothing!" said Juriga, coughing, "only your poor wife, if she should meet your son on the mountainside, would she know him?"

"Know him? No!" groaned Martin, "and how could she know him? She forgets everything else when the terror comes over her, and she wanders away crying his name on the mountainside, seeking for a little lad of a year and a half, dressed only in a little shirt; and today the boy would be nine years old."

Juriga coughed again, and tried to speak, but he seemed to have something in his throat.

"Listen, Martin! I've never told you the details of Palko's history. All you know is that my friend Rasga, left his boy with me two years ago, but I didn't tell you his story."

Poor Martin sat spell-bound, as Juriga began to talk, but when he came to the finding of the child on the mountainside Martin leapt to his feet staring wildly at the old man, and, as he finished and the full truth dawned upon him that Palko was his own son, he threw himself on the ground crying and laughing in turn, and then finally lay quite still.

Juriga rose and left him alone. Starting down the mountain path with his hat in his hand, and his eyes lifted reverently heavenwards, he went in search of Palko to send him to the chapel house, for he had not forgotten his promise. Juriga thought it best that Palko should go away to the village, and give Martin time to break the news to his dear wife in the easiest way possible, for he was afraid a sudden shock would be too much for her.

He found Palko and Martin's wife with Dunaj, busy as usual among the strawberries. "Palko mine, you must hurry down to the chapel house. Father Malina is not at all well, and is calling for you. You, my daughter, come home with me. It is time to prepare the dinner."

"Grandfather!" said Palko, "you have been to the chapel house already this morning?"

"Yes, my son, and the priest wishes to see you at once. He is very ill, and I have promised him that you would stay for a little while at his side. We shall manage without you for a time."

"Dear Grandfather," and Palko joyously kissed his grandfather, who this time took him tenderly in his arms, as he said good-bye to him.

"Now go, and take good care of him."

He was about to leave when Martin's wife caught hold of him.

"Where are you going? Where are they sending you?" asked the poor woman anxiously.

"Don't keep him, my daughter," said Juriga, "he will soon be back."

"Are you leaving me again, Palko?" she asked nervously.

"Auntie, it will be all right," said the little boy tenderly to the poor distracted woman.

"Yesterday," she cried, "you went away. I don't know where! Your presence is so necessary to me! If you go away again, I fear you will never come back like my poor Mischko!"

"No, no, never fear, Auntie! Let me go this once, for Father Malina needs me so badly. After that we shall be together always."

"Hurry now, Palko." Poor old Juriga could hardly control his tears. Palko was away like the wind!

"Let us go, my daughter, and get the dinner ready, for Martin will soon be coming home." And Juriga led her gently up the mountain.

"Why did you send Palko away?" groaned the poor woman, beside herself. "Don't you know I cannot live without him?"

Suddenly an idea shot into the old gentleman's mind, and he turned on the poor woman saying: "Why do you want to keep him here, seeing you do not care for him?"

"Not care for him! Not care for him! Who told you such a thing?" she cried.

"If you truly cared for him so much, you would stop looking for your own child on the mountain! and you—you had better look for your Mischko!"

"Oh, give me Palko! Give him to me!" cried the poor woman, stretching out her arms.

"Well, then, if I give Palko to you it will be on condition that you stop looking for Mischko. Do you understand? If I give you Palko, will you stop for ever these useless searchings of yours?"

"Yes, oh yes, I will, I will," sobbed Martin's wife. "If Palko is to be mine for ever, I will cry no more for my poor Mischko!"

"Well, here we are home and here comes your husband for his dinner," Juriga said, as Martin appeared round the corner of the hut at that moment.

"Martin!" cried his wife on seeing him, "Just think! Palko's grandfather has given the boy to us! He has had to go down to the village for a day or two—but," she beamed at her husband, "he says he'll soon be back!"

Martin bent and kissed his wife tenderly.

"Juriga has done well to send him away this time, my dear wife, and truly he'll soon come back, and he shall be ours, and we shall keep him for ever. But we owe an enormous debt of gratitude to the priest. Oh, that the boy may be able to pay something of it for us!"

The Crown of Righteousness

Palko's wish had been fulfilled for once again he found himself with his dear friend. But how different now their friendship from the days on the mountainside — no more happy excursions through the green carpeted valleys; no more long climbs to Sunshine Valley; not even a moment's chat through two long days. Yet the boy felt an exquisite joy and profound gratitude to the Lord and to his grandfather that he should be allowed the privilege of even being near his friend upon his bed of pain.

The doctor had at first tried to shut Palko out as a troublesome and useless intruder, but the priest would not agree.

"Let me have Palko here. He is my small companion. Show him what you want done for me, and he will do whatever you wish. The other people make too much noise, but you can hardly hear him when he moves."

So they let him stay, and later the doctor had to confess he had been mistaken in his first judgment. Palko did, and did well, whatever he was ordered to do. It was not much work, for it consisted largely in giving ice to the patient from time to time, and in opening and closing the window. When anything else was desired, all he had to do was go to the kitchen. Coming to and from the room he made no more noise than a fly, and he knew how to open and close the window so softly that the patient was hardly aware of it. He preferred to stay near the bed, and when he saw that the sick one suffered much pain, he prayed that his dear friend might be spared such suffering.

The priest himself prayed, asking earnestly that the Saviour might heal him, if it should be his will, and let him serve him still.

"Why, then, does he not grant our request?" said Palko puzzled. "Why does it seem as if he does not hear? And yet I am certain that he hears us!"

Father Malina asked him to read a bit from the book, but the passage chosen seemed strange to Palko. When he had finished, the priest said: "Yes, truly I have built on this foundation, 'wood, hay, stubble,' and all will be consumed. Did it pay to live and do such a useless work? I myself shall be saved; yet so as by fire! There is no crown for me! If I could have but lived and worked with the Light that I now have. What will the Lord do with such a useless servant as me?"

Palko could not get the words from his mind: 'He himself shall be saved; yet so as by fire'—'yet so as by fire'! There were so many, many things yet that he could not understand.

That night, while Palko slept, the priest fell seriously ill, even worse than before. The doctor never left him for an instant. By morning the face of the sick man was as white as the snowy pillowcase on which he rested, and his weakness was extreme. Nevertheless, when Palko drew near, he smiled tenderly at him.

"Don't be worried about me any longer, Palko, I am much better, for the weight that pressed me down has disappeared, also the pain in my side, and now I can speak without pain."

"You do not suffer any more? Well, then, the Lord has answered, and all will be well soon."

"Yes, Palko, he has. Last night death was very near, but this morning he has shown me something very precious from his Word. Read to me," and Palko read: "Henceforth there is laid up for me a crown of righteousness, which the Lord, the righteous Judge, shall give me at that day; and not to me only, but unto all them also that love his appearing."

"By this," said Father Malina, "I know that the Crown of Righteousness is for me, and is given freely, not by my merits or righteousnesses, or for any good things that I have done, but by the merits of the Son of God, Who is MY RIGHTEOUSNESS, and then, besides, it's for those who 'love his appearing'—and, oh, how we would love to see him, would we not?"

The priest spoke in such a faint voice that Palko had to lean quite close in order to catch the words. Then he asked the boy to read to him the first eight verses of Psalm 62. "Truly my soul waiteth upon God: from him cometh my salvation," and Palko read on quietly: "He only is my Rock, and my Salvation; he is my defence; I shall not be greatly moved."

"My Palko! What a grand blessing to be able to say that with certainty," said the sick man, after which he slept.

From that day, in spite of warnings from the doctor, the priest insisted on seeing his parishioners who came to visit him. Quickly the news spread, and they began to arrive, asking him to see them.

"You are going to kill him by asking him to speak to you!" said the worried doctor.

When Father Malina heard this, he took him by the hand. "Tell me frankly, doctor; how long shall I be able to live if I do not say another word?"

"That's difficult to tell," he replied.

"Let us say, perhaps, some weeks, if I obey all your instructions. Is it not so?"

"Yes, but if you keep on the way you are doing, it will be but a few days."

"May that be as God wishes. Good reason, then, to prepare for that time in the best possible way."

"Pray for me, Palko," he said, "that the Lord may grant me power to show these my people the true Way of Eternal Life before I go." And the Lord heard the fervent desire of his dying servant.

To his people who came flocking to see him he said: "It is a dying man that speaks to you—and it is your pastor as well, so you may believe him. Good works cannot save your souls, and the saints have no power whatever to prevail in heaven for you. Christ Jesus is he who paid for our ransom on the Cross of Golgotha, and his blood-God's blood, is the only thing that cleanses us from all sin. He suffered and died in our place. Christ is the Lamb of God that taketh away the sin of the world. He has taken away and forgiven all my sins, and he can take away and forgive your sins also. All you have to do is repent and turn from your sins to God, and believe the good news that 'God so loved the world, that he gave his only begotten Son, that whosoever believeth in him should not perish, but have everlasting life'."

During the second week another lot of Bibles arrived, which Father Malina ordered to be distributed to his congregation. "Never allow," said he to every one that received a copy of the Holy book, "anyone to take this book away from you, no matter who he may be, for," he added with anxiety, "it is the Eternal Word of the Living God. Read it line after line with faith and prayer, and put into practice what it says, and it will show you the Way of Eternal Life, the Life with God for evermore, as it has shown it to me."

"Palko!" he said once. "I find it hard to realize that the hour is so near when I shall see that One 'Whom having not seen ye love; in whom, though now ye see him not, yet believing ye rejoice with joy unspeakable and full of glory.'"

"Oh," sighed Palko, "if I could only go with you!"

"No, Palko mine, content yourself with serving him faithfully here on earth with all your heart. What would I not give to have served him all my life? One happy day in the future we shall be re-united in the Father's house, and you shall then tell me if my people have read God's book, and have found the way to the Sunshine Country. Be thou faithful unto death and he shall give thee the Crown of Life!"

Palko finds his Father

It was the second Saturday after Palko had come to take care of his beloved friend. The chapel house was sheltering many guests in addition to Palko, and all the regular members of the household. There was the priest's sister who had come; then there was another young priest who had come to take Father Malina's place in the church for the time being.

"Palko, as I am not so lonely as I was, it is but right that you should go and get a little mountain air into your lungs, and also bring happiness to your loved ones in your grandfather's house," said the priest. "Come back to me on Monday, and give my love to all the dear friends both at the forest guard's house and at your own home. Also, please give my best regards to the beautiful mountains, which my eyes shall never see again, and if you do get a chance to go up to the Sunshine Valley, just look again for that door to heaven, which we once saw, and remember that I shall soon pass through its gates to where, beyond the clouds, lies our true Sunshine Country."

Before going to either house, Palko climbed to the Sunshine Valley. Many, indeed were his thoughts as when, crossing the greensward by the cave, he came to that mossy seat where, for the first time, he and Father Malina, had opened the book together. Never, never would he see him here in this place, the most beloved of all spots on earth to him! Never more would he be able to sit at his friend's feet and hear him explain the wonderful mysteries of God! How sad everything around him appeared today; the birds were silent, not a single butterfly was to be seen, and even the sun itself was hidden behind some dark clouds. A storm evidently was brewing, but Palko, when suddenly looking up, saw another magnificent rainbow that appeared to be the very door of heaven. How wonderful, how lovely it was, and how beautiful it must be on the other side of that door! Alas, how high up it was! Palko felt that, once that door was shut behind his beloved friend, he would never be able to return again. Then he remembered the Saviour's promise to come again and receive his people to himself, and also what had followed in his reading that morning in the fourteenth chapter of John: 'Where I am there ye may be also.'

"Lord Jesus," said Palko, "take me along with him please! How lonely I shall be when he is no longer here. Grandfather is very old, and he, too, will soon go as my Grandfather Rasga did, and then what will become of me? Father Malina was going to have me in his house if Grandfather should die, but now—where shall I go? Believe me, dear Saviour, I do want to go with him to be with you always. Now, when I find something new and difficult in the book, to whom can I go to have it explained to me?"

The lightning still flashed above his head, and the thunder echoed the passing storm

Father Malina had told him the story of Elijah, whom the Lord had loved so much that he sent a chariot and horses of fire to carry him to heaven, and now Palko believed he heard the clamour of those chariot wheels. He was going to see those heavenly doors swing wide to allow the celestial chariot with its heavenly team to descend and carry his friend to heaven. But the sun soon shone out triumphantly above the storm clouds; little by little the rainbow disappeared, and once more the Sunshine Valley was flooded with a blaze of glory while a few drops of rain fell.

Palko had on his new suit which he had worn constantly at the chapel house. He ran quickly to the cave in order to shelter from the shower. He did not enter the cave, however, for he saw a man within, whom he had never seen before, and who was wandering about examining all the corners. Seeing this, the boy's interest was aroused, and forgetting for the moment all his sorrow, he said, in the common mode of greeting in Czechoslovakia: "What are you looking for, Uncle?"

The stranger turned round and politely returned the boy's greeting. "What am I looking for? Tell me first if you know who is in the habit of coming to this cave?"

"Who comes here?" said Palko, surprised. "Well, there's my Uncle Martin, he's been here once. Then there's Father Malina, who has visited the cave three times, but he'll never come again," said the boy sadly, "and then there's myself. It's my cave!"

"Your cave?" said the stranger laughing.

Palko looked at him. He looked like a labourer in search of work.

"How long has it been yours?" asked the young man, quite seriously.

The boy hesitated, puzzled.

"Well, sir, it's written in the book: 'All things are yours', and Father Malina says that means that God has given all the earth to men. Besides, I have asked Jesus for this cave, and he has given it to me."

"Well, all I can say is," said the stranger smiling, "that my master and I lived in this cave for four years, but I don't remember whether we asked God for it or not."

"You have lived here?" and Palko took a step toward him.

"Well," continued the young man, "my master was sick, and the doctors had recommended him to live on the mountain. He also wished to be alone with God, but he took me with him to look after him. We had a bed of moss and some blankets, and in this way we lived quite comfortably. My master recovered strength and, if it had not become necessary to return to the city, I believe he might be living here still but he, poor man, is now resting in his grave in lower Hungary. I am only a wandering mechanic, and it just occurred to me, in passing this place, to come up to see if a certain book still remained, which we left here, but I find that it has disappeared. It must have been found by someone who has taken it away."

"Here it is!" exclaimed Palko, taking it from his pocket.

"Have you read it line after line, as my master recommended on the first page?" said the stranger.

"Yes, indeed, we have," said Palko, with his earnest eyes fixed on the stranger's face. "We have read it line after line; we have put our confidence in the Lord Jesus, and we have found the road that leads to the true Sunshine Country. Your master, then, had found it, too?"

"Well, you'd have difficulty in finding a person who knew the way better than he did," and the young man sighed deeply.

"He died, and when he left you, did he go up to heaven in a chariot of fire? Has he already seen the

Lord Jesus, and the beautiful country? I shall ask Father Malina, when he dies and they meet each other there, to thank your master for his kindness in leaving us the book, and for showing us the way to read it. And you, too, I suppose you have found the way to the Sunshine Country?"

"Me? No, I'm afraid not! I was on the track of it once, but I've wandered far away since then. He gave me a copy of the book, too, but I no longer read it. May God forgive me," and there were signs of distress in the young fellow's voice.

"How did you come to stop your reading? But you seem to be sorry, are you not?" and Palko's tone was comforting. "You can begin once more to find the way. Just think! What would have become of your master, or of Father Malina, who right now is at the point of death, if they had not known the way that leads to the Lord Jesus? But come! I must go home to my grandfather's hut. I will ask Uncle Liska to give you a place in his house — he's alone, and there is plenty of room, for I've slept there often. You can tell us all about your dead master, for we have all wanted to know who and what kind of person left the book behind. As it says, there is nothing hid, but it shall be uncovered."

"Or, better still," said the stranger, "as my master was so fond of quoting, I have it still by heart: 'My Word that goeth forth out of my mouth: it shall not return to me void, but it shall accomplish that which I please, and it shall prosper in the thing whereto I sent it'."

They soon arrived at Liska's cabin, but they were so busy talking that they would have passed it, had not Dunaj rushed out with joyful yelps to welcome the return of his young master.

"There, there, that will do, Dunaj!" cried Palko. "I know you love me very much, and I love you, but you'll spoil my good suit if you don't stop. Be a good dog now and stop it, I say!"

Dunaj's barking brought Martin, who was visiting Liska, to the door, and then what a joyful welcome Palko got. Soon the stranger was introduced to Liska and Martin, and when his identity was discovered, great was their interest in the story of the good man who had left the book in the cave.

"You are welcome to stay here with me, stranger," said Liska. "With an introduction such as this, you can help me in my work until you find something to do that is more in your line."

"Now," said Martin, "we must be on our way, Palko and I, for the folks at home will be waiting to see him, and besides I have a load to carry that he can help me with. So good-bye until tomorrow."

As they started down the path together Palko said: "But, Uncle, where is the load we are to carry?"

"I'll show you presently," said Martin, taking hold of the boy's hand.

"Uncle!" said Palko presently, for he felt worried at the silence of the man beside him, "What's the matter? Are you sick, or what is it that troubles you?"

"Why, Palko?"

"Because you're not saying a word. Excuse me for speaking about it, but there's something strange in your manner, and I noticed the same in Liska, too."

"See here, Palko," said Martin, seating himself on a moss-covered rock, and drawing the boy to him. "Let's sit down for a bit. I've something to tell you. It's about what has happened in your absence," and Martin's voice trembled.

"Something has happened?" said Palko. "That's what I thought from the way you were acting!"

"Yes, my son," and somehow Martin seemed to have a new way of saying "my son." "What do you think? We have found our Mischko!"

"What?" cried Palko. "Tell me, where was he? Where has he been all this time? Please tell me all about it from the beginning. Where is he now?" And he clung to Martin as if he might get away before he had heard the whole story.

It took Martin all his strength not to reach out there and then and gather Palko in his arms, but he only said: "All right, here's the story. If you yourself had not told Father Malina a part of my story, and how my wife was still in the habit of seeking our boy on the mountain, I would never have known where to find my dear son. You will remember that Father Malina sent a message by you to your grandfather to come and see him? Well, your grandfather told me what he said, and so, after seven long years and more, we have at last found our Mischko. As I told you the other day, in a drunken stupor I lost my Mischko and he wandered away from me, with the terrible result that my poor wife lost her reason. Now we have the rest of the story. The next day the daughter of Rasga, whom you called your grandfather, found my little Mischko wandering in the forest near their home, and she adopted him."

"Why!" said Palko, bewildered, "what little boy? We never had any little boy like that."

"Listen, Palko! From that day to this, I've never touched a drop of liquor, and what's more, I have found here the Lord Jesus as my Saviour, and he has accepted me, I do believe with all my heart. He has pardoned me, as he did the poor publican in the Temple. But, Palko mine, do you think that my Mischko can forgive me for the terrible wrong that I did to him by my wickedness, which caused all this misery to his mother, and his separation from her for these seven long years?"

"Don't worry about that, Uncle," said Palko, taking Martin's hands. "The Lord Jesus knows how to work all that out, so don't be afraid. You see, Auntie and I have prayed that we should find your Mischko, and now you have found him; as if he has heard us, and answered our prayers, he will also see to it that Mischko forgives you. Besides, why should he not, seeing that the Lord Jesus has forgiven you? Have you asked him?"

"No, not yet, Palko, but there is another thing. He might forgive me, but do you think he could love me?"

"Of course! Why not, when you're his father? He'd be a funny boy if he didn't love his own father. If I had a father I'd love him, I can tell you! But I never knew either my father or my mother. I think they must have died before I could remember them. Grandfather Rasga never told me much about them. Oh, but I'm so anxious to see Mischko, where is he?"

Martin could stand it no longer. "He's here beside me now, my boy," and he gathered his child in his arms; "Oh, my son, my son!" he cried between his tears, "my beloved son! And you do forgive me, don't you?"

"And so," said Palko, bewildered indeed, "you mean that I — I — " he faltered — "I am Mischko! Oh, Father, my dear Father! I have a father after all!" Long and fast the father and son clung together.

"Now, come let's find your mother. She's waited too long already. And she knows the whole story. You'll find her different. In these two happy weeks of waiting for her son she has become her old true self again."

***

Let us draw the curtain here as that dear, beautiful mother, with shining eyes of love and welcome, comes running from the hut to greet her long-lost son! It is too sacred a scene for our prying eyes to witness, for such sights are but a foretaste of the great future day spoken of by the prophet Isaiah, when 'everlasting joy shall be upon their head: they shall obtain gladness and joy; and sorrow and mourning shall flee away. I, even I, am he that comforteth you!'

The Door of Heaven Opens

Autumn had made its appearance much earlier than was expected. An early frost had killed the last summer flowers, and the song of the birds had ceased; the swallows had flown far away to a warmer climate, taking with them the last trace of summer, and the wild geese had borne them company. On the mountainside, stripped of its green finery, nothing was heard but the hoarse cawing of the crows, beginning to gather in great companies and preparing to descend upon the crops now ready for the autumn harvest. Some of the trees were still adorned with golden leaves, but many more stood naked on the wind-swept mountain, while at their feet lay a carpet of rich colours in the fallen leaves.

It is just as on that spring day when our story opened, that we find Palko Juriga (as everybody continued to call him in spite of now knowing his true name and origin) climbing the mountainside.

The week before, at the sudden arrival of the cold weather, the woodcutters had left their frail breezy huts, and moved to the village. In moving, Grandfather Juriga had left behind his big auger* so Palko had returned to the hut to look for it.

What a silence reigned all around! Not a single hut was occupied, nor could a single human being be seen; only the rabbits ran freely hither and thither, and the squirrels sprang from branch to branch unmolested.

---

*A pointed tool for boring holes.

Palko, however, had no eyes for them, neither did he cry hallo to the echoes. His ruddy face, in its frame of yellow hair, seemed so thoughtful that he might well have stood for a model of a child in the famous picture of the Millennium days, who will lead the wolf and the lamb, the leopard and the kid, and calf and young lion together. When the lion shall eat straw like the ox, and when men shall beat their swords into ploughshares, and their spears into pruning hooks, and when nation shall not rise against nation, neither shall they learn war any more, when the whole earth shall be full of the knowledge of the Lord as the waters cover the sea.

What was Palko thinking about? Well, it seemed as if he had plenty to ponder upon. Just as the reader, arriving at the end of an interesting book, sometimes turns back the leaves to visit again the scenes and incidents he had read about, so Palko was reviewing all the wonderful things that had happened in those few short months since that spring day, when he had climbed the mountain to get the hut ready for his grandfather. How could he have believed, if anyone had told him then, that he would today have a father, a father that any boy would envy; and then to have a grandfather who was so changed that he grumbled at him no more, and into whose dwelling the Lord Jesus had come to stay?

Who would have believed that he should find a real true mother? And what a mother! So beautiful, and with eyes like merry stars, not at all like the poor sad creature his father, Martin Lesina, had brought to the hut that night on his return from the city. The Lord Jesus had heard the prayers of Palko and his father, and so his dear mother had been completely healed.

The previous week, Palko had told one more person the way to the Sunshine Country. This was Grandmother Lesina, who had returned with his father from the city. Their house there had been let, and the furniture brought to Juriga's house in the village, where they were all going to live together until the return of one of Grandfather Juriga's sons from America.

Grandmother Lesina had brought her spinning wheel to spin the yarn during the winter. Meantime, during the long evenings, while his mother got out the family mending, his father would read to the family out of the precious volume, which had been such a blessing to them all. How happy Palko was not to be such a heavy burden on his grandfather, who had had to work so hard for them both. Now, oh, how wonderful! He had a kind father, who was now teaching Palko his own trade, so that he could soon begin to earn his living. As these thoughts welled up within him while he climbed the mountain, he exclaimed: "Lord Jesus, how good you have been to me. It is all your doing. If we had not come to know you, things could never have turned out like this."

Having recovered his grandfather's drill, he left it in a safe hiding-place, and went on up the path for he wanted a last look at his beloved Sunshine Valley before the winter snows set in.

Arriving at the mouth of the cave, he entered to take a last look around at the precious place that had brought him so much joy and prosperity. Coming to the entrance, he gazed all about him. Although there were no flowers on the green carpet, the place held something of its old enchantment. The autumn sun that now shone out, after many days of rain and cold, was warm and reviving, and the boy's heart still felt drawn toward that little corner so separated from the world. Was it not here that that splendid Door of Heaven had opened to admit his beloved friend, the priest?

Yes, Palko now had everything on earth to make him glad and happy, but he could not think of his dear friend without feeling a heavy weight upon his heart. This day, somehow more than ever, there came to his mind those closing scenes at the chapel house.

The Monday after Palko had had the happiness of finding at last his father and mother in such a wonderful way, he had returned to the chapel house. Father Malina had rejoiced with him at having found his parents, and also listened with interest to the story of the saintly man, who never came to know what a wondrous work he had done in leaving the sacred book of books in the cave. Tuesday and Wednesday passed quietly, and the priest appeared to be a little better, so that he was able to move about in the house.

The following day the priest asked to be allowed to go into the garden and, as the weather was warm and beautiful, the doctor himself led him to a seat beside the garden path. Afterwards they brought a big chair from the house in which, well wrapped up, Father Malina seated himself while his dinner was brought and placed on a stand by his side. As his elder sister was taking away the dinner things, he said to her: "Palko is going to read to me, and then I'll just sleep here for a while."

"All right, dear brother of mine," said his sister, kissing him on the forehead. "I will take the opportunity to air your room and re-make your bed."

"May the dear Lord richly bless thee and thy children for all your kindness to me," replied the sick man tenderly. As soon as they were alone he took his Testament and said:

"Palko, read to me about our Sunshine Country."
Palko turned to that glorious chapter in the Revelation
of Saint John, and read about that wonderful city that
'had no need of the sun, neither of the moon to shine in
it, for the Glory of God did lighten it, and the Lamb is
the Light thereof' — and then he read of that 'River of
water of Life, clear as crystal, proceeding out of the
Throne of God, and of the Lamb.' After this the priest
explained the passage to Palko, ending with these words:

"But, Palko mine, of all the beautiful things that
we shall discover in arriving at our Sunshine Country,
the most beautiful of all will be he that sitteth on the
throne, Jesus, the Lamb of God."

After saying this he folded his hands and closed
his eyes, as he was in the habit of doing when he wished
to pray. Kneeling at his side, Palko leaned his head
against his friend's knees and prayed also. But as the
prayer seemed to be a great deal longer than usual,
Palko at last raised his eyes to his friend's face. The
sick man, with his head leaning against the side of the
great chair was sleeping, but from time to time he
breathed much more heavily than usual.

An indescribable feeling, solemn and strange,
seemed to fill the heart of the little boy as he watched
his sleeping friend. He hardly dared to breathe, so
careful was he not to disturb him, for now his friend
had become perfectly still. Over his face, which
hitherto had worn a look of sadness, there had come
a decided change, as if the sleeper was lost in some
wonderful dream, for to the pale countenance had
come a smile of perfect happiness.

Hearing steps near him, Palko looked up, and
seeing the young priest, he made him a sign to come
more quietly. The young priest drew near noiselessly,
but as he bent over his friend, he gave a cry that

rang through the garden. Father Malina had gone, at last, where he had desired to go — to that country where the sun never, never goes down!

Up in the Sunshine Valley, as the last scene came before Palko, his eyes began to fill with tears. All those closing moments, especially his friend's last words, were engraved in his memory, and would never be forgotten.

"Why should I cry?" said Palko. "He is so happy up there! It was the Lord Jesus that came and took him to his Father's house. Now he has seen all, and he has seen him that sitteth on the throne of God and of the lamb. He has met the kind stranger, who left the book in the cave, and who wrote those words in it, and he has thanked him heartily for me; so I am content, for some day the Lord Jesus will come to take me, too— but in the meantime, dear Lord, keep me faithful, that I may show many more the way to the Sunshine Country."

Other Classic Fiction Titles

Little Faith
A little girl learns to trust
O.F. Walton
Faith, persecuted by her grandmother when her
mother dies, finds faith and justice.
ISBN: 1 85792 567X

Christie's Old Organ
A little boy's journey to find a home of his own
O.F. Walton
Christie is a street child. He sets out with Treffy, the
Organ Grinder, to find a place of peace.
ISBN: 1 85792 5238

A Peep Behind the Scenes
A little girl's journey of discovery
O.F. Walton
Rosalie is forced from place to place with her brutal
father's travelling theatre - if only she could find a
real loving relationship?
ISBN: 1 85792 5246

Saved at Sea
A young boy and a dramatic rescue
O.F. Walton

Young Alec lives with his grandfather in a lighthouse. In the middle of a dramatic rescue attempt a little girl is saved from a shipwreck. But what else changes in Alec's life as a result?

ISBN: 1-85792-7958

The Little Woodman
An abandoned child finds a true home
Mary Sherwood

A little boy is abandond by his wicked brothers and is left to fend for himself in the forest. He only has his dog Ceasar for company but he learns that he has another friend who sticks closer than a brother - the Lord Jesus Christ.

ISBN: 1-85792-8547

A Basket of Flowers
A young girl's fight against injustice
Christoph von Schmid

Falsely accused of theft, thrown from her home, her father dead - Mary learns to trust God.
Exciting tale with a dramatic twist.

ISBN: 1 85792 5254

Other Classic

Stories

Mary Jones and her Bible
The story of a girl whose inspirational desire to have
a Bible in her own language led to the founding of
the National Bible Society.
ISBN: 1-85792-5688

Childhood's Years
An excellent collection of short stories including
the fascinating mystery, 'The Bible in the Wall.'
ISBN: 1 85792-7133

Children's Stories D L Moody
Stories used by this world famous evangelist to
teach Christian truths within his own Sunday school.
ISBN: 1 85792-6404

Children's Stories J C Ryyle
Stories for children by this great communicator
including the well-known classic, 'The Two Bears.'
ISBN: 1 85792-6390

Classic

Devotions

The Peep of Day

A popular devotional title from the 19th century.
Written by F. L. Mortimer to be used
within a family setting.
ISBN: 1-85792-5858

Line Upon Line 1

The second in the F.L. Mortimer's devotional titles.
Covers scripture from Genesis, Exodus, Numbers
and Joshua.
ISBN: 1 85792-5866

Line Upon Line 2

The third in the classic devotional series by F. L.
Mortimer. This titles covers 1 and 2 Samuel; 1 and 2
Kings; Daniel and Ezra.
ISBN: 1 85792-5912

***

Look out for the our new edition of the devotional
title: Morning Bells and Evening Thoughts
by Frances Ridley Havergal

CHRISTIAN FOCUS

Staying faithful – Reaching out!

Christian Focus Publications publishes books for adults and children under its three main imprints: Christian Focus, Mentor and Christian Heritage. Our books reflect that God's word is reliable and Jesus is the way to know him, and live for ever with him.

Our children's publication list includes a Sunday school curriculum that covers pre-school to early teens; puzzle and activity books. We also publish personal and family devotional titles, biographies and inspirational stories that children will love.

If you are looking for quality Bible teaching for children then we have an excellent range of Bible story and age specific theological books.

From pre-school to teenage fiction, we have it covered!

Find us at our web page:
www.christianfocus.com